Happily Never After

The Savanah Shadows Series, Book 1

by

Missy Fleming

F & I
by Melange Books

Published by
Fire and Ice
A Young Adult Imprint of Melange Books, LLC
White Bear Lake, MN 55110
www.fireandiceya.com

Happily Never After ~ Copyright © 2013 ~ by Missy Fleming

ISBN: 978-1-61235-559-7 Print

Cover Art by Caroline Andrus

Happily Never After
Missy Fleming

There's no such thing as happy endings.

Savannah, Georgia is rumored to be the most haunted place in America. Quinn Roberts knows it is. She's felt the presence of spirits her entire life. Only none of those encounters ever turned violent, until now. The same darkness feeding off her stepmother has promised she won't live to see her eighteenth birthday and each attack is more terrifying than the last.

Not one to rely on others for help, Quinn reluctantly lets actor Jason Preston into her life which has complications of its own. Together they try to figure out what exactly this ghost wants from her and how to stop it. What they find is the ghost doesn't just want to hurt Quinn, it wants revenge.

It wants her life.

This book is dedicated to my family, who never stopped believing or supporting me. And for reading drafts when I needed another set of eyes. I love you guys so much.

I also have to thank TL Tyson, the best friend, critique partner, and writer I've come across. Tee, you have been a great teacher and you'll never know how much its meant to me.

And for all the ghost hunters out there...you all have the best job in the world.

Prologue

Mama always told me Savannah was home to more than just the living. I remember her telling me stories of ghosts and magic, and things that normally belonged in fairy tales. Her rich, syrupy voice would wrap round me with a magic of its own, making me believe. She said all you had to do was step out onto any street and you could feel it in the air, tickling the edges of your imagination, inviting you in.

We lived in one of the oldest houses in the historic district. A tall, proud home fronted with white columns standing like guards against the unrelenting Georgia humidity. Mama said that besides her, Daddy and me, we also lived with a little boy and a soldier from the War of Northern Aggression. They crept through the house at night, moving furniture or crying. She said they even stood guard at the end of the bed. I never saw that. For me, it was always a flicker of an image, a brush of wind on my face, or the glimpse of something from the corner of my eye. I never gave them a second thought. In Savannah, you were only considered odd if your house *didn't* have ghosts.

I was seven when Mama died of an aneurism. She once told me our loved ones never truly left us, and those words were a comfort to me during that confusing time. At least they were until late at night, when Daddy was already asleep, and the shadows pulsed around me in their silent dance. Those shadows made me wonder what happened to her.

One night, as I watched the shadows dance, I wondered where she truly went. To my child's mind, if the city were as haunted as she said, she must still be there somewhere. All I needed to do was find her.

The following mornings, on my walks to and from school, I searched for her everywhere. I investigated the slightest breeze or tiniest movement of the bushes. Every night, when my house fell silent, I wandered through the rooms asking for her. When I saw something out of the corner of my eye, I begged

1

them to find Mama and bring her back where she belonged. Each time I felt cold fingers walking up my spine or the hair on my arms and neck stand up, I whispered 'Mama' into the darkness.

In all my years of searching, I never found her.

Chapter One

When the principal called for 'Quinn Roberts', I walked across the stage to accept my diploma and expected to feel some kind of accomplishment. All I got was an overwhelming sense of relief.

Graduating high school should've been one of the happiest days of my life. Not only was I leaving behind the snake pit of hormones and torture they called a high school but, like any kid, I dreamed of this day. I was supposed to be on the verge of having all my dreams come true, surrounded by family and looking to the promise of the future. Instead of dreams and rainbows, I stood in the sweltering heat with my classmates and feeling more alone than ever.

My stepmother, Marietta, hadn't bothered to come or at least pretend to care.

"I'm so glad it's finally over." Abby, my only friend, came over to stand by me after the ceremony. "If I never see the walls of that hole they call a school again, I'll be the happiest girl alive."

This made me smirk. Anyone looking at Abby wouldn't think 'happiest girl alive' as a first impression. Her long blonde and pink hair fell in a straight shot down her back but it was her heavily lined eyes, the nose and lip piercings, and black fingernails that set her apart from the hordes of perfect little Southern belles roaming Savannah High.

I wasn't much different, only my hair was black with some recently added purple accents and I had no facial piercings. Abby and I bonded over our uniqueness in our freshman year and stayed friends through the endless taunting and teasing. Our loner status wasn't the only thing we had in common. We were also both being raised by single parents. The only difference was her mom actually cared.

I draped my arm over her shoulders and said, "Yep, today we can

3

officially begin life in the real world. No more nasty things written on our lockers."

"No more stupid rumors spread by your lovely stepsisters."

"I thought the one about how we put a curse on the basketball team was pretty inventive."

"Yeah," Abby snorted, "especially considering we've never even been to a basketball game. That team could have used a little magic."

My stepsisters, who were juniors, ran with the typical 'popular' crowd. Their favorite thing in the world was to make my and Abby's lives miserable. From spreading rumors about us being lesbians or devil worshippers to spray painting 'witch' on our lockers. Those kinds of things happened every single week. We were smart about it, though. We kept our heads down and counted the days until graduation.

I shrugged my shoulders, put on my heaviest Southern drawl and said, "What will we ever do without them?"

"Get on with our lives, like normal people?"

We turned from the hugging and picture taking and walked away. I felt out of place, and enormously sad, in the midst of everything I'd lost. I glanced over my shoulder at the happy families and found myself suddenly envious of the kids I spent the last four years avoiding and fearing. They were surrounded by families who actually loved them and they could think of the future and those stupid rainbows. I was grateful I'd been allowed a mere two hours of freedom to come to my own graduation.

Abby's mom came for a while, but had to leave for her second job. I considered her more of a mother to me than Marietta. She tried to help as much as she could, but to be honest I've never told her how bad things really were. I wasn't sure she'd believe it. I didn't think anyone would.

"Do you really have to go back to work, Quinn? Can't you blow off the wicked witch for a little while longer?" Abby whined as she picked at her black and pink fingernail polish.

I grimaced at the thought of going back to Baubles, Marietta's over-priced and overly pretentious beauty salon in the Historic District. "Remember what happened last time I disobeyed a direct order."

Abby flinched without saying another word.

She believed I had every right to contact family services, but I didn't see the point. Marietta had never done anything physically to me. Her specialty was making me feel less than human. At least I only had to wait until the end of the summer to be done with them. The second I turned eighteen I planned to move out.

"So anyway, I heard this story the other day about a guy up in North

Carolina who caught an image of Bigfoot on his thermal camera. It belly crawled into his camp and stole a candy bar. It's a true story, I swear. Although, I'm not sure what confuses me more; the fact there was a Bigfoot in NC, crawling around on his belly commando style, or that he'd take a candy bar of all things."

Abby never failed to distract me with her strange and random stories. In the last few years, she'd become a master at it. We parted ways a block from Baubles and I hadn't even gone fifty feet before I recognized a familiar stirring beside me.

Cold breath surrounded me but instead of frightened, I felt comforted. In the five years since Daddy died, I'd come to rely on the strange presence more and more, especially since it seemed to take pleasure in tormenting Marietta and her daughters whenever I was punished. Unlike the other spirits who seemed confined to the house, this one followed me everywhere. Even with all my research, I had no clue what it was or what it wanted.

The presence left before I entered through the back door of Baubles. I took a couple seconds to revel in the blast of air conditioning but it didn't take long for my peaceful moment to be interrupted.

"What took you so dang long?"

Marietta's high, annoying drawl always made my heart beat a little faster. Lately, I'd sensed a strange dark presence around her, a clinging shadow. It ebbed and flowed, and even pulsated with her moods. What disturbed me the most was how it seemed to be getting worse, darker somehow. That, and the feeling it had something to do with me.

"I finished Suzie's talent costume," she continued, "so I need you to go over it. Snip off the loose threads and check the seams. Then, you'll cut out the pattern for Anna's costume. Also, the floors need sweeping and wash the towels. Oh, and restock everything for tomorrow. I've left you a list for home, too."

And then she was gone, leaving a rank cloud of jasmine perfume in her wake; no congratulations, no questions about graduation, nothing. I sighed. No matter how often it happened, her indifference and cruelty still hurt. Back when she started dating Daddy, she was charming and loved to laugh. It all changed with one fatal heart attack.

I only hoped I wouldn't have to deal with her daughters today as well.

"What are you standing here for, freak. You heard her." No such luck.

Annabelle came out of the large storage room that we currently used as pageant central. She had the same white blond hair as her mama, but instead of teasing it into a gravity defying mess, it flowed past her shoulders soft and shiny. Without a doubt, the twins were beautiful but their cold attitude and nasty demeanors made it very hard to see.

"Yeah, get to work," Suzie mirrored as she posed beside Annabelle with her hand on her hip. Her hair was shorter, layered to her shoulders. "You think you get to relax because you graduated today? Mom told us that next year when we graduate we're going to have the biggest party this town has ever seen."

"Bigger than our Debutante party." They'd had one of those ridiculous 'coming out' parties where they were launched on the poor unsuspecting young men of society. Marietta used the allure of our family name and our history to push her way into the snobby circle of women who really ran this city. Of course, they ordered me to stay in the back with the help when, in all reality, it should've been my party as well. Not that I wanted to be shown off like a piece of meat.

I ignored them and walked into the storage room. Rising up to their challenges never turned out well for me. I could stand up for myself when I had to but they were masters at waiting a couple of days before striking for something I didn't remember. The last thing I wanted to do was make my day-to-day life any more difficult. An all out war would have only one casualty— me.

I started going over the hideous costume for Suzie's so called talent of tap dancing. The layers and layers of tulle were supposed to transform her into an old west saloon girl, but I couldn't see it. Instead, she was a cross between Madonna and a cotton ball. The twins went back to practicing their walks on the other side of the room.

They were competing in the Georgia Southern Miss pageant held in August. I hated pageants and everything they stood for, which meant I actually thought they stood a good chance of winning. Everything I found lacking about our society and our preoccupation with beauty showed in the twins. They were a perfect example of 'beauty is only skin deep'.

On the other hand, their talent and walking skills were amazingly awful and it took everything inside me not to laugh openly when they rehearsed

Movement near the door caught my attention. Marietta stood just outside the room and something drew my eyes to hers. I almost shrunk back in revulsion.

There was such an intense hatred coming from her as she looked at me. Behind her, the shadow rose up and expanded. The heavy smell of river water, musky and wet, drifted towards me and I fought the sensation of not being able to catch my breath, like I was drowning. Overcome by a paralyzing fear, my body began to shudder in response.

"You will never see your eighteenth birthday, Quinn Roberts."

I jumped back in shock and knocked over the chair, pressing myself

6

against the wall. Vaguely, I noticed Anna looking over and muttering 'loser' before turning her back on me.

The raspy, female voice echoed through my mind as Marietta kept her eyes trained on me. My instinct told me it came from the strange thing I sensed clinging to her, but why would it want to cause me harm?

Then, just as sudden as it started, Marietta broke eye contact and walked away. In the next instant, everything went back to normal. A quick glance told me the twins were completely oblivious.

I couldn't stop shaking or get my heartbeat to calm down. It pounded against my chest in a savage beat. My terror and the lingering smell of putrid water were the only hints of what occurred.

The room started to spin and I knew I needed to get out of there. With my mind set on breathing some fresh air, I hurried out of the room. As I passed through the doorway, I heard a faint splash and looked down.

A small, murky puddle was on the floor right were Marietta had stood. Cautiously, I bent down, dipped my fingers in it and brought them up to my nose. It was exactly what I'd smelled in the room. I flicked the tiny drops off my fingers and ran outside. The bile shot up my throat, taking me by surprise and I barely had enough time to bend over before being sick.

When I finished, all that lingered was the cold rock of fear in my gut and the realization that someone or something wanted me dead.

Chapter Two

It was nearly midnight before I finished all my chores and finally had a chance to make a sandwich. I took it upstairs so I could eat while curled up with a book I found in the public library on hauntings.

After the events at the salon, I really needed to try to relax. I'd been tense and anxious all day, jumping at shadows. No matter how hard I tried, the stale taste of terror didn't leave my mouth and throat. Invisible eyes followed me everywhere. I hoped the book would have something about what I'd experienced. There had to be a way to defend myself if it happened again.

I had a feeling it wasn't over.

Mama turned out to be right about Savannah and the older I got the more I grew attuned to it. It took a lot of energy for a spirit to manifest so it wasn't often that I saw an actual being. I knew the difference between a mere breeze and the presence of something spiritual. Occasionally, I caught a personal detail but mostly, it was a wave of emotion. I could tell them apart, too. Some filled me with sadness. I sensed their anger, their hatred or their need.

I finished my sandwich and closed the book, it was impossible to concentrate. Nights like this, I immersed myself in the history of what I'd found in the attic. It was nice to get lost in the lives of other people in a different era.

The day before, I came across a small old trunk full of yellowed letters, birth and marriage certificates and other important papers. Since I was too restless to do anything else, I got up and pulled the trunk over to my living area. I grabbed a notebook to catalog what I found and made myself comfortable on the floor. Mama had been a widely known archivist and historian. It's something she must have passed on to me because I couldn't get enough of it.

A slight rustle stirred the space beside me and the humid night air cooled to an almost uncomfortable temperature. Out of the corner of my eye, I saw the very faint figure of a small, black boy. Mama always mentioned being aware of his presence and how she came to count on his company when she found herself alone. Even Daddy, who grew up in the house, told me about the boy and how he'd come to rely on the boy's comforting friendship.

I tried to watch as he sat on the floor beside me. If I looked at him straight on, the image disappeared. As far as I could tell, he was about seven or eight years old and wore tattered clothes. He always calmed me or made me feel content. When I was a little girl, I named him George. The truth is, I might never find out his real name, but that didn't stop me from talking to him.

"Hey, George, you'd think since I worked my butt off today and graduated high school and had my life threatened I'd be dead tired." I grinned. "Sorry, about the pun. I'm just excited to see what kind of stuff is in this box. It's a welcome distraction from this thing earlier. I don't really want to talk about that. I glanced at the dates last night and it's the 1870's and on. Wonder if that was when you lived?"

A cold pressure appeared on my arm, as if he'd laid his hand there and I caught sight of him nodding his head. Reaching into the trunk, I pulled out a stack, savoring the musty smell and the dry, wrinkled feel of the century old papers

"These are letters, to a William Jennings from Catherine Roberts. That would have been one of my ancestors." I paused to read a couple. "She's thanking him for helping her family out and she's talking about their upcoming marriage. But it just doesn't sound the way a woman who's about to be married, the wording sounds too polite and stiff, even for those times. Which means it must have been an arranged marriage."

The dates on the letters and Catherine's mention of this man's assistance made me wonder if William helped our family out during the Reconstruction.

When Savannah surrendered to that jerk General Sherman, he stopped his burning of the South and spared the city. Still, it wasn't safe. The War had bankrupted the once proud South and the people of Savannah were hurting. I remembered reading about how the Roberts' cotton empire crumbled after the War. Maybe this William guy gave them a loan.

"Oh, here's a wedding announcement for William and Catherine. And her death certificate, less than a year later. How sad."

I picked up another stack of more official looking papers. The first was a letter addressed to the law office of James Owens from the Roberts family attorney. I read aloud.

"While the Roberts' family understands your grief during this sad time, they regret to inform you, again,

9

that they will not accept your offer to purchase the home on Lincoln Street.

"The Roberts estate has always passed to the daughters of the family and while you were married to Catherine for the length of ten months, she still has a younger sister, Daphne, who will stand to inherit in Catherine's absence. As her husband, you do not have any legal right to the home and not being a citizen of the South, would not understand our traditions.

"Your numerous and increasingly large monetary offers are appreciated but wasted effort at this time. Mr. Roberts and his wife will be eternally in your debt for your previous assistance in such a difficult time but have absolutely no interest in selling their family home."

This William Jennings guy must have thought himself entitled to the house after Catherine died. It made me wonder about the circumstances under which Catherine married someone who was obviously a Yankee, which back then was almost a crime.

Daddy once told me about how the Yankees flooded the South once the War ended. They swarmed like a bunch of buzzards, circling over the remnants and picking off those who were hurting the most. Even though they resented the Yankees, the Southerners were forced to work with them. It was the only way to stay above water financially and be a part of the rebuilding. Some of the older families held on to their grudges still, as if their lives depended on it.

Absently, I mumbled aloud, "I wonder how William took the news about not getting the house."

I found my answer in the next letter, a hand written attachment to the one I'd just read from the family's attorney.

"I feel it is my duty to warn you, Mr. Roberts, that Mr. Jennings' demands and requests appear to be more desperate with each attempt. He has ceased communicating to me through his lawyer and has called on me several times in person. You know what kind of man he is, sir. I must warn you, do not think him an irritation that will soon go away.

"You knew my aversions concerning the union of your eldest daughter to a Yankee from the beginning.

Regardless of what you thought you owed him, I feel he will not be satisfied until he has finished your family. The mysterious circumstances involving Catherine's death should not be ignored.

"Please, as I believe for the safety and prosperity of your family, we must find a way to pacify him before it becomes too late."

I blew out a breath. "Did you hear that, George? The 'mysterious circumstances' of Catherine's death. This William guy must have been a real mental case."

In answer, the letter I read blew off the stack, revealing a newspaper article so brittle and faded it was hard to make out the words. After studying it for a few minutes, it became hot to the touch.

The article mentioned the unexplained disappearance of William Jennings, who was last seen leaving his home. After days of searching, the authorities believed he met an unfortunate end. On a related note, at the end of the article, Mrs. Margaret Roberts, mother to William's deceased wife, was treated for 'emotional exhaustion' and was being watched by doctors following her breakdown.

My mind refused to settle on one detail. There were *way* too many unanswered questions. I noticed George no longer sat beside me. Once again, I was completely alone in the attic. A part of me wondered what the connection was between Catherine's death, William's disappearance and Margaret's breakdown.

I attacked the papers in the trunk with determination but after another hour of scouring every piece, I found nothing. Finally, I felt sleep trying to pull me down and I decided to give up for the night. Tomorrow, I'd have a fresh eye and see if I missed something. Also, there were the other trunks to go through. One of them might have more papers, and answers. I loved puzzles and mysteries and this was turning into just that.

As I lay in bed thinking back to what I learned, I couldn't help but think the papers were only the beginning. Maybe I'd spent too much time believing in ghosts and spirits, or maybe I'd inherited Mama's curiosity, but something told me I was meant to discover those documents. I wanted to learn more about why Catherine agreed to marry an obsessive sounding Yankee and how exactly she'd died.

The minute I thought her name, a pressure pushed down on my chest. There wasn't anything but darkness. No light, not even the window or my computer screen was visible in the room. This was darkness on a whole other level and it terrified me. The sickening scent of old water from earlier pushed in from all sides. It made me realize I knew this darkness.

The weight on my chest got heavier. Then, to my horror, cold fingers slowly wrapped themselves around my neck. I wasn't sure at first if the cold stole my breath or the invisible fingers were choking it out of me. I panicked. No matter how hard I tried, my arms and body resisted, refusing to do anything. I was frozen and not just because I couldn't move. A chill, colder than anything I'd ever felt, shrouded me in its embrace. White puffs of my gasping, waning breath stood out in stark contrast next to the blackness.

My mind wanted desperately to fight, but all I managed to do was open and close my mouth like a dying fish, struggling to get air. Even the silence pressed me down. My effort to draw breath made no sound at all. I thought my imagination had taken over because for a second I heard a raspy female laughing, but it flitted in and out of my consciousness too quick to make sense of.

I sensed my body shutting down. I had no idea how much time passed. Inside I screamed, wanting to live, but all I was aware of were those icy hands on my neck and everything fading. I knew the precise moment I stopped fighting because a strange peace came over me, and I almost welcomed the spots in front of my eyes. It meant I wouldn't have to stare into that horrible darkness any more.

Before I gave myself over to death, a bright white light flashed out. It lit up the entire attic and for a brief second, I saw what held me down. There weren't many details that I caught in the quick flash, but I saw eyes and a mouth both darker than the mass itself, endless voids into another place. The light expanded and blinded me, forcing me to close my eyes. After another second, it was over.

I opened my eyes and took a heaving breath. I still felt the after effects of the fingers on my neck but at least I could breathe again. The deep, ragged gulps of air calmed me and my heartbeat slowly returned to normal.

The light faded and dimmed. Whatever came into the attic and saved me was already leaving.

"Wait," I managed to say, the word sounding like a weak gasp. "Who are you?"

Nothing answered me. The normal nighttime darkness returned to the room and I sat there, savoring the ability to breathe and listening to the sounds of the house. The thing that attacked me must have left or at least it had been beaten back by the light. I had no idea what just happened. My mind wasn't able to grasp the fact that I'd almost died.

The reality hit me almost as hard as the presence had. Sobs ripped through me and I curled up in a ball on the bed. All the suspicions I had recently pondered about something dark in the house became blindingly real.

Fear forced me up off the bed and around the attic in a panic, turning on every single light. I went back to bed and threw the covers over my head, like a terrified child. For hours I fought exhaustion, I didn't want to be asleep and defenseless. The last thing I remembered before my eyes closing was whispering 'thank you' into the brightly lit room.

Chapter Three

I tried to avoid asking Marietta for anything. More often than not she shot me down before I even started. But I needed to get to the Georgia Historical Society to do some research. I had a hunch that if I found out more about Catherine and William, I'd discover who or what I might be dealing with. There was no arguing they were connected. I just needed to find out how.

Whatever happened yesterday scared the crap out of me and I wanted answers.

At eight o'clock, I went down to the kitchen and found her sitting at the breakfast bar, sipping coffee and reading the paper. The dark shadow swirled, expanding the farther I walked into the room. Even the faint smell of the river, which I was getting used to, reached out to greet me. I remembered the shadow looming above me, holding me down and I fought my instinct to turn and run. Something told me that's what it expected but I wouldn't give it the satisfaction.

"Good morning, Marietta. Can I get you anything?" As much as it made me sick to even pretend to be nice, I wanted to keep her in a good mood. It didn't help matters that my whole body tensed and I held a fight or flight stance.

"You don't have to play the good girl, Quinn. If you want something, just ask."

This took me by surprise so I blurted out some of the truth. "I wanted to spend some time at the library today. If it's okay with you, of course."

Suddenly, the shadow grew behind her and the air in the room changed. It became cold and charged, how it is during a thunderstorm. I froze, fully expecting a repeat of the attack. Before I knew it, all the cabinets and drawers in the kitchen slammed open and shut, making me jump and squeal. Marietta

14

sat there passively as if nothing happened.

I barely had a chance to consider running as half a second later the air changed back to normal and quiet settled over the room, probably because Suzanna and Annabelle chose that moment to appear.

"Don't you have something to do besides bother us?" Anna asked as she sauntered past. She left the smell of strawberries in her wake and I found it funny considering it was such a pleasant smell coming from someone so unpleasant.

"I was asking Marietta a question," I replied softly. Today wasn't the day I wanted to attract their attention, not with the dark presence so close.

"Then get out of here. I don't want to ruin my breakfast," Suzanna said as she walked by and rammed her shoulder into mine.

"Omigosh, I forgot, did you hear about the movie they're filming here this summer?" Anna blurted out as she grabbed a banana out of the fruit bowl.

Suzie shook her head while Marietta kept her eyes focused on me.

Anna continued, "They're filming a movie right here in Savannah! A vampire movie, you know based on all those books? And guess who's going to be Brandon, the dark moody, vamp? Jason Preston."

This time Suzie squealed and grabbed her twin. I rolled my eyes at them as they started jumping up and down.

Everyone knew who Jason Preston was and even I allowed myself a half second to go all dreamy. Tall, dark, and mysterious, he played the black sheep in the long running family drama, Home. He had this cocky smile that made every girl want to find out what he was thinking.

I shrugged away the frivolous thought. What the heck did it matter?

"You may go to the library," Marietta announced loudly, "just keep your phone on in case I need you. The girls and I are having a mother-daughter day with shopping and lunch and a movie. Sometimes you need to be with *family*." Another dig aimed at me. "Also, we'll have lasagna for dinner tonight so make sure you're back early enough to make it."

Not wanting her to take it back, I scurried out the door as the girls protested against letting me have any free time. More and more Marietta had been forgetting to have me do my normal cleaning and housework. Granted she, or the thing controlling her, possibly wanted to kill me, so who cared about chores?

Finally, outside in the bright morning air, I was able to take a deep breath.

Whenever something paranormal happened in the house, Marietta's first reaction was to scream and cower in another room. She had sat there while the cabinets opened and closed without batting an eye. It confirmed she must not be aware of what was happening to her.

I texted Abby and told her to meet me at the Historical Society, that I had some interesting things to tell her.

I truly believed something I found last night triggered the violent response from the shadow. I needed to figure out what and why. The vaguest hint it had something to do with Catherine tickled the edge of my mind. She died and her husband of barely a year disappeared without warning. Something didn't add up. Plus, there was the female voice I thought heard.

The Georgia Historical Society was located in the WB Hodgson Hall on Whitaker Street and housed over four million manuscripts, 100,000 photos and thousands of portraits and artifacts from the very beginning of Georgia's history. The light brown building didn't look like much from the front but the inside it was a site to behold. The high vaulted ceilings made the reading room feel even bigger than it already was. I always loved the smell of history in the air, the musty pages of books guarding their secrets.

I walked up to the information desk and asked for records on Catherine Roberts or William Jennings from the 1870's to 1890's.

Abby arrived as I began sorting through the stacks of material a library aide had set down.

"I'm here, what are we looking for?"

I quickly took her through the events since leaving her yesterday, trying not to make a big deal over the attack. Abby saw right through my vagueness.

"You've got to be kidding me. You *have* to get out of that house, Quinn. What's it gonna take for you to get that?"

"It's my home, Abby. I don't know how else to explain it. I need to be there for something. I only have to make it a couple more months. You understand more than anyone what the house means to me."

She sighed heavily and leaned closer. "I do but I'm worried about you. I think you're expecting magical things to happen when you turn eighteen. We've both learned life doesn't turn out that way."

"I've spent the last five years of my life scared to stand up for myself. If I don't learn to do it now and find out what exactly is going on, I'll never escape it."

"That completely makes sense Q, but what you're forgetting is that something might be trying to kill you. You get that, right?"

Instead of answering her, I concentrated on the reading in front of me. She got the message and started in on what appeared to be a stack of ledgers.

We sat in silence for a long time and then Abby straightened in her chair, waving to get my attention.

"Quinn, I found something about Catherine Roberts. It's the meeting notes for a group of women who called themselves Saviors of Savannah. They were dedicated to getting the city back on its feet after the War. Anyway, they made mention of Catherine's body never being found and the officials finally issuing a death certificate. She had been a member up until she married then 'dropped out of sight', abandoning them for a 'life of pampered Northern privilege'."

"They never found her body? One of the letters last night mentioned her husband was suspected in her death before he disappeared." I didn't know what I expected to find but something didn't feel right. "I wonder if either Catherine or her husband, William Jennings, is controlling Marietta?"

Abby's eyes got real big. "That's quite an assumption to make."

One of the things I loved and hated about Abby was she always had to be the voice of reason. It didn't matter that she believed in ghosts as much as I did or considered herself an amateur ghost hunter; she still looked at things from a very logical angle.

"Marietta didn't turn into a crazy person until Daddy was gone. Before he died, she was annoying and spoiled but never malicious towards me. I didn't notice the presence hanging around her until after, which makes me think there's significance there. Plus, it's getting worse, resulting in an attack on me last night after I found papers talking about William Jennings and his suspected involvement in his wife's death. His wife, who happened to be a Roberts."

"Okay, I'll admit it makes sense the evil spirit in your house could very well be this Jennings guy but I don't see the connection of it being Catherine."

"I don't either yet. I heard a creepy female voice. Maybe she had a strong connection to this house like I do. Maybe he killed her and her spirit is looking for some kind of revenge. It still doesn't explain why I wouldn't be seeing my next birthday."

"It's possible. I think we need to do more research first."

We didn't find much else, except for records of Jennings' business deals and more mentions of Catherine's disappearance and how it affected her family. One thing was extremely clear. In a time when most of the South was bankrupt William Jennings had been one of the richest men in the country. Jennings had his finger in everything from real estate to shipping to manufacturing. During the War, when the ports were blockaded, his ships were the only ones allowed in and out because of his contacts in the North.

He would have made a fortune in the South had he lived.

I left Abby and rushed home to get dinner in the oven. Marietta ordered it to be ready at a certain time and I didn't want to push my luck today, not so soon.

It wasn't until nausea had me in its grips that I realized I'd passed in front of the house with the green trim. My mind had been so occupied I forgot to block the sight I'd see otherwise. Now, all I could do was put my head down and not let it take me over.

An icy blast hit me and I knew she was there – the woman on the lawn. Her whimpers drifted into my consciousness, but I did not turn to see. The heartbreak wafting off her was almost enough to bring me to my knees. She'd haunted me since I was a little girl, not because she followed me, but because the front of her nightgown was stained with blood. Her wrists were slashed and the image was seared into my mind forever. I didn't have to look to feel her desperation.

Then, she whispered the anguished words she always did. "He w-was going t-to leave me."

Swallowing thickly, I picked up the pace. Love scared me. Everyone I'd loved had been taken away from me. There wasn't anyone to take my hand and explain why it turned ugly or desperate, to tell me that one day I'd meet a guy and all my beliefs would change. Considering everything else that was going on, the idea of meeting anyone of the opposite sex seemed silly and remote.

Chapter Four

A week later Marietta sent me on a mission to find some kind of frilly fabric for one of Anna's dresses. Things had been unnaturally quiet since the incident in the kitchen and I'd been so on edge I didn't even have the urge to do any research into Catherine and William.

Pageant errands were the bane of my existence. I lost track of how many dresses each of them needed, they were all so big and ruffled and ridiculous. I always assumed most girls bought their dresses but Marietta was a talented seamstress and insisted on making theirs. According to her, it made Anna and Suzie stand out even more. In my opinion, it made them even more spoiled.

After already trying two of the fabric stores in town, I decided to try one a little closer to the waterfront.

The waterfront and old downtown were my favorite parts of Savannah. I took my time strolling down the sidewalk and studying the buildings. It was such a pretty city but what gave it that creepy, yet almost magical feel, were the trees. Tall, drooping trees, draped in Spanish moss were twisted and gnarled from hundreds of years. Thick, green 'town squares' dotted the neighborhoods nearest the river and I always compared it to living near the forest. You didn't have to walk far to find a large open park and plenty of green space.

Every free second I had, I spent taking pictures of the trees and the squares. Right now, I had enough to make a very impressive coffee table book. Photography gave me the chance to escape. When I looked through a camera, the world disappeared. Along with it, all the taunting, and the sadness and the being ordered about faded away. Then, all I was left with was the object in my viewfinder. The simple plays of light and dark, the brutal honesty of the image, it helped my world make sense even if it's just for that second.

Staring across the street at a particularly massive live oak and considering how I would capture it in the best light, I didn't see the person standing right in front of me. The collision would have knocked me off my feet if someone with a strong pair of arms hadn't held me upright.

"I'm so sorry, I'm such an idiot…" I started before getting a really good look at who still had their arms supporting me. It was Jason Preston. I couldn't believe it and the shock struck me speechless.

He didn't say anything either, just smiled at me with that little dimple in his chin and his dark brown eyes sparkling, dark hair falling across his forehead. He was even hotter in person.

I noticed a couple beefy guys nearby watching me like a hawk and assumed they were security.

"You okay?" he finally asked. I still couldn't think of anything intelligent to say so all I did was nod. "Good, you were looking around like you're lost. Are you lost? I'm not from here, but I can pretend and help you find your way."

There was the cocky grin I remembered from TV.

"Are you flirting with me?" It was such a ridiculous thought and saying it aloud really made me wish I were anywhere else. I heard my voice and recognized the snarky tone, as if I found the idea of him flirting with me repulsive.

He let me go and looked at the ground as he laughed. "Maybe but I'm not doing a very good job at it, obviously."

"I'm from here. I was just looking at the trees." There, I said something even more idiotic. I expected him to run away at any moment and not spare a single glance backward.

Instead, he turned towards the tree I'd been staring at and cocked his head to the side.

"I can see why, they're very mysterious. Like sad old ladies draped in veils." That surprised me. It was the last thing I expected him to say. "It makes sense that Savannah has the kind of reputation it does."

"Reputation?" I got the uneasy feeling I normally got when people started talking about my home. It was hard to listen to them wonder or mock the presence of ghosts when I'd felt them my entire life. Most of them treated it as a novelty or a tourist attraction.

"Yeah," he looked back at me. "They say it's the most haunted city in America. I'd love to find out for sure while I'm here doing this movie. I'm Jason, by the way." He held out his hand.

I heard a squeal come from the end of the block and knew he'd been spotted by his adoring fans.

"I know who you are." I stared at his hand without taking it, vaguely aware it was rude. The whole conversation felt a little surreal to me. My brain completely stopped working which didn't help with trying to find something to say. "My stepsisters are crazy about you."

He lowered his hand and tucked them into the front pockets of his jeans. He flashed the cocky grin again. "Are they as beautiful as you?"

With a shake of my head, I rolled my eyes and walked away.

"Seriously?" He called after me.

"Yep," I answered over my shoulder as I saw a group of girls running towards him.

"Where do I find you if I need another cruel shot at my ego?"

It was hard to not answer him. I kept on walking but his laughter followed me the rest of the afternoon.

I didn't have much experience with boys, but not from lack of interest. Seeing how the boys at school bowed to my stepsister's whims I knew they weren't for me. I hated the fact that Jason did all the stupid cliché things like making my heart speed up and my palms sweat. I growled in frustration.

When I reflected on the five minutes I spent with Jason, I couldn't help but feel a little disappointed with myself for not even attempting to be charming and with him for being almost exactly what I expected.

I finally found the fabric Marietta sent me in search of but it had taken much longer than it should have. Luckily, when I made it back to Baubles, she was with a customer and in full suck-up mode. To make matters even better, the twins were also out and it was Saturday, which meant it was my one night to go out, my one night a week I had with an extended curfew.

Hoping not to upset Marietta any more than necessary, I took extra time with my chores to make sure there wouldn't be anything worth complaining about.

"Quinn?" My head jerked up at the sound of my name. It was Mrs. Hoppel, my high school English teacher and head of the Photography Club.

"Hi, Mrs. Hoppel, what brings you here?" I caught Marietta watching me intently.

She patted her short grey bob. "I'm getting a little trim. I wanted to congratulate you after graduation but I wasn't able to find you."

Mrs. Hoppel had always been my favorite teacher and taught me a lot about photography. I considered her my mentor in a sense.

"I'm sorry. It was so crazy I must have missed you." She was another one of the people I cared about who had no idea what life was like at home. Oh, I'm sure she heard about the trouble I got at school but that was different.

She reached into her large tote purse, pulled out a couple brochures and handed them to me. "These are some schools I wanted you to look at. This first one, obviously, is Savannah College of Art and Design. I know how much you love living in the city so I assume it's your first choice. It's getting down to the wire for late applications so you might want to do that soon. If you haven't already, that is."

I knew she was trying to be helpful but it made me uncomfortable. There would barely be enough money for me to set myself up somewhere new let alone start any kind of college. Going to SCAD was my dream but I didn't see it happening. I took the brochures from her and smiled.

"The other one," she continued, "is for the Hallmark Institute of Photography in Massachusetts. I understand the idea of going to the North and those frigid winters is appalling to any of us Southern women but this is an excellent school. Maybe you want a change of pace."

Marietta hovered nearby, not even making an effort to conceal her eavesdropping. I'm glad Mrs. Hoppel didn't notice her because she would have launched into an embarrassing conversation about my future.

I thanked Mrs. Hoppel for giving me the information and walked her to the front door of the salon. When I turned, Marietta ripped the brochures out of my hands.

"I'll take these. You won't need them." She sneered and walked away, leaving her awful jasmine perfume behind. I tried to ignore the faint musty water smell hiding beneath it. The scent scared me a little.

Later that night I went downstairs to remind Marietta I was leaving. She and the twins were in the family room watching a recorded pageant as if it was the evening news. For a brief flash, I had a vision of how the room used to look.

Once upon a time it was full of pictures of me, of our family. Now if you looked through the house, you'd find no proof of my existence. They hid me away like a dirty secret.

"Just wanted you to know I was going out, Marietta." Anxiety slicked over my skin, I never knew what kind of mood she would be in or more important, what her mood towards me would be.

"Fine, remember be back by midnight." She tore her gaze away from the TV and fixed me with a look of malice. "Don't forget what happened last time."

Before I could answer she turned back to the TV, dismissing me.

Walking out I heard Suzie yell, "Have fun with your lesbian witch friend."

All three of them laughed as I closed the door.

Chapter Five

I stood on the sidewalk and took a deep breath. For the next five hours, I was free.

Abby had succeeded in roping me into doing amateur ghost hunts with her for the last few months. She was the only person who knew about my so-called ability. Her theory that I was some kind of sensitive or medium made me uncomfortable but it didn't stop me from wanting to learn more.

Until now, we had only conducted our little experiments in my house, when everyone else was gone, or at the old restaurant where Abby's mama worked. I sold a couple first edition books from the attic without Marietta knowing and bought the kind of equipment we saw on TV; a digital voice recorder, a video camera with night vision and a still camera as well, which I also used for my photography.

So far, we thought we'd come up with some pretty great evidence – multiple shadows and voices from various parts of my house and one really impressive piece of video footage of what appeared to be a shadow person. No matter how many times we caught something significant it took a long time for me, the girl who sees ghosts, to admit it wasn't a fluke or an explainable shadow. Holding a piece of evidence that showed the hidden world I saw everyday sobered me.

Mostly I had the option of pretending the ghosts I saw were all in my head. Investigating with Abby stole that from me little by little.

Tonight, we were going to Colonial Park Cemetery, Savannah's oldest burial ground, to try some of our equipment outside. Abby said we needed to step up our game and the Old Cemetery would be perfect. Even though there were only about 600 markers present, we heard rumors that close to 9,000 people were buried there. That kind of atmosphere made it a perfect place to try to contact restless spirits.

The waning moon peeking through the clouds made it exactly the kind of place a ghost would call home. Savannah had a way of turning from beautiful to straight out of a horror movie in seconds.

I saw Abby standing at the gate to the cemetery. "Hey girl, you ready?"

She grinned at me and held up our bag of equipment. "I'm always ready. I have a feeling this is going to be awesome."

We picked our way to the oldest part. Drooping trees sheltered most of the cemetery and the crooked crumbling tombstones were like a drunken army standing watch. Already I knew we were not alone. My consciousness began to sense various spirits nearby. I tried not to let the atmosphere dictate my reactions. It was still easy to spook myself considering everything else going on lately.

"This looks about as good a place as any. I think we're far enough from the street that we shouldn't have any noise interference."

I stopped under a giant tree and Abby pulled out our cameras. It surprised me that even in the middle of a busy city, the silence could be so thick and complete. I couldn't hear anything. Wispy clouds passed over the moon and threw strange shadows all around us.

Off behind a large tombstone, I watched one shadow move in the opposite direction of the others. Learning how shadows fall and react to light was important and I knew from experience this particular shadow was different. If I opened my mind, the emotions and desperation of the dead would overwhelm me. I read stories of people claiming to be sensitives who couldn't step foot in a cemetery or a battlefield or even a funeral home. Thank goodness I was slowly learning to tune it out, sort of like switching a channel.

Abby handed me my expensive still camera. I attached the infrared lens and started snapping pictures while she began recording. No matter how many times we'd done it, starting one of our investigations, as Abby called them, gave me the feeling of being on a rollercoaster, on the big hill teetering over the edge.

During the first couple attempts, I felt silly asking questions to the dark, asking someone who might not be there to make themselves known. Familiarity came with practice and now I didn't think twice about asking a spirit to identify itself. Especially after getting some very convincing answers back.

Abby had just asked if anyone was there when I heard movement from behind us. It wasn't a couple random footsteps. Something big was coming towards us in the grass and not gracefully either. Abby must have heard it, too, because she swung the camera towards the noise.

"Are you coming towards us?" I asked loudly, hoping to catch the EVP, or voice, of whatever was out there.

No answer.

The movement was closing the distance between us with each passing second. My body tensed and every single one of my senses became heightened. I knew something was about to happen so I took a small step back and glanced at Abby. She had the video camera trained on the spot and returned my look with alarm. Normally, I'd be able to get a feeling if there was anything nearby. I had no idea why this was different. In response, my breathing picked up.

"Hello?" Abby asked, this time I could hear a slight tremor in her voice.

"What are you doing out here? You scared me to death." A cautious voice called from the darkness.

We looked at each other in confusion as a figure stepped out from behind the tree. I wasn't sure who was more surprised to see Jason Preston—me or Abby.

He looked between the two of us before finally recognizing me.

"You again?"

I couldn't help it. I started laughing. Slowly, Abby and Jason joined in, letting out their relief. Abby was the first to talk.

"How do you two know each other? And why didn't you tell me about it, Quinn?"

"Quinn," Jason smiled. "Finally I discover the name of the girl who left me standing in the street like a jackass." He turned to look at Abby and said, "She ran me over earlier while looking at trees, accused me of flirting, then walked away leaving me standing there with my wounded pride."

Abby chuckled, "Sounds like Quinn."

"So what, did you follow me?" I asked him.

He raised his eyebrows in surprise and laid a hand on his chest. "Me? I'm more the being followed kind of guy."

"Oh, please." I went to walk away. Something about him irritated the crap out of me and set me on edge. All I wanted was to be away from him so I could breathe and ignore the signals my fluttering stomach was sending out, especially when he looked so good in his skullcap and dark sweatshirt.

"See, she's always walking away from me. It hurts. Now, really, what are you girls doing out here? Séance?"

Thankfully, Abby was also the kind of girl who wouldn't go all gooey at the sight of a hot actor. "A séance, are you for real? We're conducting an investigation." But I heard the way she tried unsuccessfully to sound professional.

Great. Not only does he think I'm a crazy girl who stares at trees, now he thinks I hang out in cemeteries at night searching for monsters.

It didn't matter that both of those things were true but it did make me feel more freakish than I already was. Then I remembered I didn't want to impress him anyway and tried to throw a bucket of cold water on my thoughts. Why did I have to run into an actor, of all people?

Jason scrambled to keep up with us. "An investigation? As in, searching for ghosts?"

I figured it couldn't get any worse. Maybe if I told him the truth he would think we were crazy and leave. I stopped and faced him.

"Yes, as in ghosts. You've seen the ghost hunting shows on TV, right?" He nodded. "Well, that's what we're doing, kinda, only on a very amateur level."

His eyes lit up with interest. His reaction wasn't what I expected.

"Have you found anything? Is there someone you're looking for? Can I help?"

I almost groaned. The expression on Abby's face wasn't quite readable. It appeared she was as perplexed as I was when she blurted, "I can't understand why you'd want to help us."

"I came here for the same reason, only without all the equipment. I can't imagine anyone coming to a city like this and not being curious about what's out there. So, have you ever seen anything?"

"Maybe," I began simultaneously as Abby said, "We've got some great stuff."

Jason looked at me with newly found respect. "So you guys are the real deal? Cool."

"I don't know if you can call us that. Again, we're amateurs. And we're done for the night."

Abby's eyes widened in surprise but I knew she wouldn't argue with me as she packed up her camera. Jason's enthusiasm was a little more than we'd bargained for.

"Well, can I tag along next time? I'm curious about this sort of thing." He watched as we gathered our supplies.

Abby stood up and got really close to him. "And you think two girls like us are the kind to show you? Maybe we're here for something very personal and don't need some actor butting in."

"Maybe I am too," he said softly.

That caught my attention. I couldn't imagine what he thought could be found in a cemetery at night. The last thing I wanted was have him see even a glimpse of anything personal to me. But when I peeked at him, I saw a familiar shadow of pain in his eyes, which made me feel a little selfish.

I slung the duffel bag on my shoulder and pointed behind him. "If you walk in a straight line that way, you'll find the south gate."

Abby and I left him standing in the darkness, staring after us. It wasn't until we reached the street that Abby finally said something.

"I can't believe that just happened! I mean, that was who I think it was, right?" She walked into a nearby late-night coffee shop and took a seat.

"Unfortunately." I settled across from her and ordered a hot lemon tea. I'd never developed a taste for coffee. "He's kind of a jerk."

She snorted. "Yeah, but an incredibly *hot* jerk. Was he serious about how you met him?"

I took my long hair out of its messy ponytail and shook it out. "Yeah, I literally ran into him on the sidewalk and he tried his 'I'm so charming and hot and famous' thing but I'm immune."

"I saw that with my own eyes," she giggled. "I bet he's never had a teenage girl walk away from him before."

The giggling seemed to be contagious because I started as well. "At least I won't have to see him again."

Abby raised an eyebrow. "You think? He did seem pretty determined."

"I don't want to consider that." I sat back in my chair. "The last thing we need is some stuck-up, pretty boy getting in the way."

"I don't know, Q. Maybe it would help. The way he looks, I can't imagine even a dead woman being immune, even though you seem to be."

"I've never been attracted to giant egos. It really is a shame he showed up tonight. Our investigation was a complete waste."

"Not a complete waste," Abby said as she drained the last of her coffee. "At least you were able to get out into the real world for a couple hours."

Later at home, I sat down at my computer to watch the footage we'd taken. In the brief time we were at the cemetery, we'd accomplished nothing. This didn't really surprise me considering we'd been interrupted before even beginning.

Satisfied I was safe and no one would see, I logged onto the internet and Googled Jason. I couldn't help it. Something about him and the sadness that appeared in his eyes as we were leaving made me incredibly curious.

I found out the basics. He was twenty-one and had already left a trail of heartbreak through young Hollywood. He originally came from Colorado before hitting it big and avoided any major scandals. Sure, he'd donated a lot of hours working for Habitat for Humanity and Big Brothers, Big Sisters but it didn't take away from the fact that it was everything I expected to find. I got bored with it pretty quick.

Right before I signed off I saw what it was that could explain his sadness. It was an article in the Denver Post five years ago, about a year before his first acting gig on *Home*. Jason had been driving up to go skiing with his younger brother Dylan. They were in an accident and Dylan died.

A car swerved into their lane and Jason hit a patch of ice trying to avoid it. Dylan died at the scene before emergency vehicles could reach the remote area. A brutal picture formed in my mind of Jason on the side of the road holding his brother as the life slowly drained from him.

Unwanted tears filled my eyes. I had assumed he knew nothing about pain and loss. How horribly wrong could I have been? To be the one left behind, to be the one left living, affected a person in more ways than one. This was why he was so curious about Abby and me hunting for ghosts. He must want to try to reach his brother.

It made me wonder how much of his cocky attitude came from that day, how much of it was to hide his hurt. Much to my chagrin, I found myself wanting to help him. I felt horrible now about the way I'd treated him.

Maybe, I'd have a chance to make it up to him. All I needed to do was keep my ears open and find out either where he was staying or where the movie was in production.

From the corner of my eye, I saw a shadow move at the far end of the attic and felt comforted. I watched as it pulsed and moved almost peacefully towards the door.

If Jason was searching for answers, I doubted I was the girl to give him any. I didn't care how annoyingly good looking he was, he still rubbed me the wrong way. I made the decision to find him as soon as I could and offer to help him. Hopefully that would ease my conscience. The sooner I tried to help him, the sooner I would be rid of him.

Chapter Six

The thing about summer in the South, especially in Savannah, is it catches you by surprise. Though I have lived here my whole life, I was never fully prepared for when the force of the heat, mixed with the thick, wet blanket of humidity arrived. July came crashing into the city like a runaway freight train.

For a month, I tried to find Jason. I searched the places we'd previously met and where the movie was being filmed, but I never got close enough to see him. In the end I appeared to be only one of a hundred pitiful girls waiting for him to strut past. I was close to giving up. Let him find his own answers.

Today, Anna and Suzie, who were also hanging around the movie set, caught me trying to get close to the fancy trailers. Before I could slip through the crowd and out of sight, they saw me.

"I can't believe you're here," Suzie taunted. "Either you're pathetic and hoping to catch a glimpse of Jason Preston or you're meeting some of your fellow vampire freaks."

Shame flooded my face as she pointed to a group of scary looking Goth kids I'd never seen before. Better they thought that than the actual truth.

Anna stepped closer and bumped into me. "You better leave before we tell Mom. I'm sure she won't be happy about you being here and not at home working."

"I saw a crowd and came to check it out," I squeaked out.

The only thing I hated more than feeling humiliated or that I didn't fit in anywhere was the rush of meekness that washed over me whenever the twins were near. They had a way of making me feel small, like I was an intruder in the life that, by rights, belonged to me as much as it did them. Their constant reminders that I was the outsider had eventually become my reality.

I learned to live with the teasing and the flat out mean attitudes but their taking my place, in my life, beat me down.

Suzie lifted up the full cup of iced coffee she held and dumped it over my head. The cold, sticky liquid dripped into my eyes and down the front of my shirt. I hung my head and frantically tried to cover the thin shirt, which was now see-through, making the peace sign bra perfectly visible. Tremors raced down my body as the embarrassment flushed through me, making me painfully aware that my cheeks and neck had probably turned a deep red.

To make matters worse, I heard a commotion closer to the set and looked up in time to lock eyes with Jason. I turned and ran the moment I saw the recognition flash in his eyes. I didn't stop running until I was blocks away and despair crashed down on me.

I wanted to run home and throw myself in the arms of my loving mother. Closing my eyes, I let the fantasy wash over me and tried to ignore the stabbing pain of loss. She would wrap me in a hug and whisper that everything was going to be okay, that I was better than those girls were. Then, she'd kiss my forehead and we would go into the kitchen arm in arm to bake cookies.

I knew, as I opened my eyes, it was a childish fantasy but in that moment I would've given anything to make it come true. My heart ached for it. My heart ached for her.

Gathering myself up, I made my way to Baubles and tried to steel myself for my reality.

Even though I cleaned myself up as best as I could, Marietta still threw me glares all day. My hair was matted to my head and eventually she ordered me to wash it in one of the sinks. Afterwards, it was easier to pretend the nightmare of Jason seeing me in that condition that never happened.

As I got back to work, I watched Marietta closely.

There was no denying that her clients loved her. She knew what they wanted and how to make the most common and plain women feel beautiful. Even the inside of her salon reflected the tastes of the woman I once knew. I'd call it understated elegance. The walls were a deep red complimented by gold trimmed draperies. Wood floors added to the warm feeling as did the muted lighting and soft, antique furnishings. Marietta forced me to work there but over the years I grew to love it. Under better circumstances I would have enjoyed the experience.

When Marietta catered to her clients I saw the woman Daddy fell in love with, the woman who at least acted happy to be in the same room with me. After Daddy's heart attack five years ago, it all changed. Any sentiment she expressed towards me as a daughter vanished with him.

It didn't matter that something controlled her or, as I started to suspect, possessed her. Her change of heart still hurt, more than I cared to admit.

Occasionally, as I watched, I got a sense of the shadow thing. I was wondering if it was stronger at the house when the twins interrupted. I braced myself for a continuation of the incident earlier.

"Mom! Mom! He's throwing an actual masquerade ball out at that new fancy resort. And he's going to be a guest judge at the pageant." Suzie squealed at the top of her lungs.

Marietta came out of the back. "What are you talking about, sweeties?" She laid a hand lovingly on each of their cheeks.

"Jason Preston. In honor of the movie, he…" Anna began.

"His studio," Suzie chimed in.

"Fine, his studio is throwing an old fashioned masquerade ball, with costumes and masks and dancing. In the spirit of the old South or something like that. And he's judging the pageant! You have to find a way for us to go to the ball so he can meet us."

"Oh, that won't be a problem at all. The resort manager's wife gets her hair and nails done here once a week. I'll make the arrangements."

"You should go lie down, Mom. Do you have one of your headaches again?" Anna asked as she inspected Marietta closely.

Marietta's response was lost to me as I let my mind wander into dangerous territory, into a hope I never thought I had before.

I pictured myself in a beautiful gown waltzing with Jason to the envy of everyone. I felt so accepted. The room sparkled, the faces of the people looking on blurred as we moved past. It reminded me of Mama's fairy tales and even though I knew it was stupid, I found myself uttering damning words. "It would be fun."

All three of them stopped talking and stared at me as if I'd grown a horn in the middle of my forehead. Then, they erupted into hysterical laughter.

Marietta was the first to recover. "You? At an actual ball? With actors and important people? That's the most ridiculous thing I've ever heard. Who do you think you are? You don't belong anywhere near this ball."

Suzie walked up and got in my face. "You'd be the laughing stock of the entire evening. Look at you! Have you seen the way you dress? This is a classy masquerade ball, not a devil worshipping convention for sluts."

I froze as they put me in my place. I knew I had crossed a line for even trying to hint that I wanted to be part of their world or seen at the same public event as them. Studying their hateful faces I remembered the coffee incident earlier and something inside me snapped.

"If I really was a devil worshipper don't you think I'd have done something awful to you a long time ago? Do you think I enjoy the three of you tormenting me all day, every day?"

There was no warning for the slap that cracked across my face. Before I had a chance to recover, Marietta took a handful of my hair and yanked my head backwards.

"You are an ungrateful child! Instead of sending you to family services and foster care, I let you live in my house. I felt sorry for you so I kept you."

"The only reason you keep me around is because Daddy's will ordered you to! And it's not your house!"

She threw me on the ground and stood over me. "The minute you move out, I'm selling that evil house. Oh, you look surprised at that. I realize you plan to leave at the end of the summer when you turn eighteen. So you have a choice, your freedom or your precious house. Once you leave, I can do whatever I want to it, maybe even burn it to the ground."

The darkness leapt up behind her and rushed at me. The cold breeze pierced through me and shattered my flimsy courage. Something vile coursed inside my body and all I wanted to do was throw up. From a distance I heard one of the twins complaining about the air conditioning being too cold. Then, as quickly as it started, it was over.

For the second time that day, I ran away and hated myself for it.

She knew exactly how to play me and I let her. She knew how strongly I felt about my family and how much I loved our house. The surge of hatred crashing through me was something I'd never felt before. It scared me a little. When I finally took note of where I was, I saw I had stopped at Colonial Park, where Abby and I ran into Jason.

Stumbling through the gate and past some surprised tourists, I made my way deeper and deeper into the sea of tombstones. Even after being attacked by a spirit of some kind on these grounds, I knew I would find quiet acceptance here. No one would hurt or disappoint me. I came to the same tree where we met Jason and sat down at its base, trying to calm down.

The comforting presence of a familiar spirit settled next to me. It was the one I felt so often and the one that saved my life. Cold surrounded me and I almost got the impression of arms hugging me. I closed my eyes and let myself relax.

"Are you okay?" a voice asked.

Opening my eyes and turning towards the sound, I saw it was Jason of all people. The presence disappeared instantly, leaving me a little disoriented. I'd gone so far down today it didn't even faze me that he was seeing me in this state. My eyes were probably red and puffy from fighting the urge to cry, one cheek redder than the other because of Marietta's vicious slap. I wondered briefly if I looked better with coffee spilling down my face.

I nodded wearily at him as he sat down beside me.

"I saw you earlier," he whispered.

"A glimpse of my charmed life... I'm fine, just another typical blowout with my evil stepmother and stepsisters."

Jason laughed softly at that. "Evil stepmother? What does that make you? Cinderella?"

"There are days when I think I have more in common with her than anyone could imagine." He studied me skeptically. "Never mind. What are you doing here again?"

A slight shrug of his shoulders was all I thought I'd get in reply but after a few seconds he answered, "I wanted to make sure you were okay. Had a hunch to try the cemetery. And maybe I'm here hiding from something, looking for something."

Then I remembered the story I read about Jason and his brother and how I wanted to help. The best thing I could do was change the subject from me to him, a subject I was sure he loved.

"The night you ran into us here you said you wanted to see what it is we do. Are you still interested?"

In his eyes I saw a flicker of something resembling hope.

"Okay, I'll warn you, I'm far from an expert but I can answer some of your questions and show you how we use what little equipment we have. Do you have any plans for the rest of the day?"

"No, I'm done with filming for today. It's a vampire movie so a lot of my scenes are at night but I'm free until tomorrow."

I stood up and brushed off the back of my shorts. "Good, I'll have Abby meet us later with the equipment. First, I need to go somewhere and it's kind of personal. Do you want to come or meet me later?"

My polite Southern manners betrayed me. Inviting him along had not been part of the plan.

He studied me for what seemed like an eternity. "Let me go with you, if that's okay. I don't want you to conveniently forget meeting me later," he joked. "Besides, it seems like you could use a friend."

My traitorous heart leapt so I turned and headed out of the cemetery. This wasn't the moment to get all gooey-eyed. After what Marietta had said about the house, I wanted to find Daddy's old partner at the law firm and get some answers. Right now, he would be the only person capable of helping.

Chapter Seven

Jason and I walked in silence the two blocks to the bus stop. Martin Bradley had been a partner in Daddy's law firm for as long as I could remember. After Daddy died and Marietta cashed in his half of the partnership, Martin opened an office in a newer part of town. I hadn't seen or talked to him in years.

Only a few people we passed on the way to the bus stop seemed to recognize Jason. Or at least they gave him a second look that said they recognized him from somewhere but couldn't quite place it.

The most impressive part to me was he didn't even seem to notice. In fact, the more time I spent with him, the more I believed his cocky movie star attitude was a bit of an act itself. He appeared perfectly content walking alongside me and not caring where we were going. It was unsettling and dangerous.

I had to keep thinking of him as an egotistical ass. It was safer that way. Even a foot away from him on the sidewalk, I felt such a strong magnetic pull between us. Pretending not to be aware of his proximity, his charm, or his looks was a fulltime activity.

He didn't seem to have any bodyguards or security following him today so I constantly expected to be overrun by a group of crazed girls.

We stopped at an intersection and waited for the crosswalk light to change. The bus stop was located in the next block. I caught the sight of our reflection in the store windows next to us.

I almost did a double take.

Jason looked the same, his normal attractive self. But my gaze didn't linger on him.

I focused on the girl standing next to him. She wasn't anything special, especially since her eyes were red and her hair was flat. The girl in the reflection didn't belong there with him. If he were the sun, she was a mostly cloudy day with a high chance of rain.

Honestly, how stupid could I be?

Martin Bradley's office was located in a modern building dominated by huge walls of glass and concrete, the kind of building I hated. It didn't fit with the rest of the city.

The receptionist told me he had a meeting in twenty minutes but she went to ask if he could see me right away.

"Quinn!" Martin boomed as he strode out of his office and wrapped me up in a fierce hug. "I'd recognize you anywhere, sweetie. Did you get the package I sent to you for graduation?"

"I-I, no I didn't, Mr. Bradley." Without saying so, I already knew what happened. Marietta must have kept whatever it was for herself.

Martin looked confused. "That's weird. Perhaps your stepmother forgot to give it to you."

I didn't want to get into family issues in front of Jason. "Can we talk for a few minutes? I have a couple things I need to ask you."

"Sure, I've got some time. Come on in."

He led the way into his office and I peeked over my shoulder at Jason who gave me an encouraging smile.

"Have a seat," Martin said as he closed the door and sat behind his desk. "Now, what is it I can do for you, Quinn?"

I fidgeted in my chair suddenly not sure where to begin. "I had some questions about Daddy's will. When he – when it happened, I was still too young to understand what his wishes really were."

Confusion crept over his face and he leaned forward in his chair. "I assumed Marietta went over it with you."

"We don't have the easiest relationship." I almost laughed that the extreme understatement. "In fact, I liked to think if Daddy had known how my life turned out, he would have made other arrangements, such as sending me to live with my aunt and uncle in Seattle."

Martin shook his head. "I don't understand. Surely, if things were that bad you would've come to me sooner or I would've heard about it. Because your father remarried, Marietta was the logical choice instead of sending you thousands of miles away. She never requested differently."

The thought of living somewhere cold and grey, the way I imagined Seattle, did not appeal to me at all. I knew I would have fought it. My mama's sister and her husband were strangers to me anyway. We hadn't seen them since Mama died.

"Sometimes it's easier to let things happen than to try and do anything about them." The sound of maturity in my voice surprised me. How was it fair that a seventeen-year-old sounded weary of the world already? "But that's not important now. I'll be eighteen in a little under a month and Marietta told me something disturbing. She said she would be kicking me out and selling the house. I planned on leaving already but I always hoped the house would be mine."

"I'm confused, Quinn. I was the executor of Andrew's will but I never had the chance to speak with you. You were too distraught."

I didn't remember much about the days after Daddy died but the parts I did remember filled me with such sadness and loneliness that it made reflecting on it hard.

"I discussed the matter with both Marietta and her lawyer. We agreed since she became your legal guardian, she would judge when you were strong enough to hear the contents of the will. Being a friend of the family, I agreed. I felt I had no reason to distrust her. I even got back the document you signed."

This made me weary. I didn't remember signing anything. "What document?"

"The one stating you heard the terms of the will and understood them. "

I had the strange and sinking feeling that Marietta had lied to me about something very important. "What did the will say, Martin?"

"I remember it vividly, as I drafted it up. Andrew Roberts willed all of his assets to his wife, Marietta. Guardianship of you also went to her as well as the house. But the house remained under her control only until you reached the age of eighteen."

It felt as if the entire world stopped in its tracks and silence descended over it. The only sound I heard was the intense beating of my heart, thudding in my chest as if I'd just run a marathon.

"I always believed the house passed to Marietta, period. In fact, that's what she told me back then and has continued to tell me for years. She never said anything about the house passing to me."

Martin looked shocked as the depth of Marietta's deception settled over both of us.

"What are the other provisions of the will, as far as the house is concerned?"

"The same provisions that have been in the Roberts family for centuries. As long as a Roberts daughter lives there, the house cannot be sold by anyone other than a Roberts without her permission."

None of it made sense. Why would Marietta lie about the house? She hated it. I was going over every scenario when it dawned on me.

"You said you had my signature?"

"Yes, give me a second to find it."

I tried to remember if I had signed anything but so much about that period of my life was jumbled by my grief. The beginning of an explanation started building in my mind.

"Here it is." Martin brought over a thick file and sorted through it. "Ah, I found it."

He handed me the document. I recognized my signature, or at least what I remembered my signature to have looked like five years ago. Then, the memory flashed vividly in front of me.

Marietta and her lawyer had sat me down and told me that everything, including the house, had passed to Marietta alone. At that age I wasn't concerned about the house and it one day being mine. I was trying to adjust to a whole new life. Her lawyer came over and sat beside me asking me to sign the document just to confirm that they shared the contents of the will with me.

I signed without reading it. Back then, I had yet to have a reason not to trust Marietta.

"It's my signature, I'm sure of it. Except when I signed this I was signing it based on what Marietta told me. She told me the house and all of Daddy's belongings were now hers. End of story."

Understanding showed on Martin's face as he began to realize what had happened.

"Martin, if I didn't know the house passed to me on my birthday and I moved away, severing all ties with Savannah, what would the result be? I mean, according to the will and its provisions."

"Basically, it's fair game if you no longer live there, especially if you didn't answer the summons to a hearing. If a Roberts daughter does not reside in the home, it reverts back to the next of kin. Who, in this case, is Marietta. It's an old addendum that has been in these wills since before the War. It's one that doesn't make much sense any longer, but no one has changed it for hundreds of years. It can be fought, of course, but this is the South, honey. You know as well as I do that our courts hold many of the old ways in high respect. Your stepmother could claim abandonment and win the ability to do whatever she chooses with the house."

"And if I were dead?"

Martin's eyes widened but he answered, "Under those unfortunate circumstances, if you yourself do not have a will, it would revert to the widow of Andrew Roberts and the guardian of his daughter."

I nodded and thought about what I learned. It was more or less what I'd begun to suspect. If I was gone and didn't realize what was going on, Marietta would regain control of the house. By not telling me, she was hoping I would want to leave and never look back. It was her final move to sever me from my family.

I wondered what role the thing that seemed to be controlling her had to do with it. It had to be connected.

"What do you suggest I do?"

"My legal advice? Don't give her any indication you know the truth. Once you turn eighteen, we can file a motion to have her removed from the house. We'll do it by the book to make sure we get the result we want, you in possession of your family home. My personal advice is to play it safe. She obviously has an agenda and I'd be as careful as possible until your birthday."

"I'll do anything if it means I can get her and her daughters out of my house. I'm sure all she wants to do is sell it and take the money. It's a prime piece of real estate. So you'll do whatever we need to do? File the necessary papers? I should warn you, I'd have no way to pay for your services."

He stood up and came around his desk to sit beside me. "Even if that were true, I would do this for free. Now, I have one more thing to tell you. I'm assuming since you've been told nothing about your inheritance, you also don't know of your mother's."

Chapter Eight

My head was already spinning with the implications of Marietta's deceit. I wasn't sure I could handle anything else.

"Mama?"

"This is something you can be assured Marietta knows nothing about, at least to my knowledge. Andrew would have told you this when he felt the time was right but I'm guessing he passed before he could." Martin laid his hand on my arm. "Your mother came from a rich family as well. She entered the marriage with her own set of impressive assets. Before you were even born, she set up a large trust in your name and she intended for you to come into this money on your eighteenth birthday. Your father shared with me that he and your mother believed this was when your adult life would truly begin."

I was astounded. Not only would I be able to keep my family's house, but also I wasn't the poor broke girl I'd always assumed.

"How much?"

"When the trust was set up, the amount was five million. After eighteen years of gaining interest, I'd imagine its well past that point, maybe even doubling or tripling its value. You're about to be a very rich woman, Quinn."

My breathing got faster and the room spun. I felt Martin patting my back in comfort but it didn't really compute. In the course of a few minutes, my entire life had changed. Even now, I couldn't bring myself to believe that it would last. Marietta, with the help of whatever presence held sway over her, had gone through a lot of trouble to ensure I'd never discover any of this.

It couldn't be this easy.

"Does Marietta know about the trust?" I whispered.

"As far as I can tell, no. I'm so sorry, Quinn. I see from the expression on your face that life has been harder than I ever imagined. Believe me, if I'd known it was as bad as I'm now suspecting, I would've done something about it. Your father was a dear friend to me."

"It's okay. You used to be a part of our family. This is a weird request, but is there any way you can check to make sure the money's still there? I don't trust that Marietta was clueless so I need to find out."

"Sure, let me make a few phone calls. Why don't you go out and wait with your friend? I'll come out when I'm done."

He walked me out and asked his receptionist to let his next client know he'd be a little late. Jason walked over and guided me to a chair.

"How did it go? You look a little shell shocked."

"I had good news and disturbing news. I'm not sure what to make of it all right now. It hasn't sunk in yet. I'll have a better idea in a bit. He's making some phone calls."

Jason shifted in his chair to stare hard at me. "I realize you don't know me that well, but if you want to talk, I'm really not a bad guy."

I found myself wanting to tell him. Trust had become a fantasy to me. It was something I wished was true, but somehow it always felt just out of reach. I didn't particularly like Jason. He annoyed me more than anyone else I'd ever met, but his blue eyes were filled with concern. Maybe it was easier spilling secrets to a stranger you never planned to see again. If he told anyone about the strange girl who compared herself to Cinderella and hunted for ghosts, who would believe him? I decided to take a leap of faith, based upon the fact that soon I'd be rid of him anyway.

"It kind of has to do with the evil stepmother. My mama died when I was six and my father remarried after I turned eleven. Then, when I was almost thirteen, Daddy died too, leaving me with my stepmother and her two daughters. I wasn't joking when I told you I had more in common with Cinderella than you'd believe.

"To make a long story short, she's made my life a living nightmare. Her daughters made my high school life even worse, horrible stuff. I thought I'd be able to leave once I turned eighteen but this morning she said if I left she was going to sell the house that's been in our family for over two hundred years.

"I learned today that when I turn eighteen, apparently the house reverts to me. It's only hers temporarily but she never told me that. She led me to believe my father willed the house to her and only her. If I moved away like I've planned, she has the right to sell it."

He laid his hand on my arm. "And she kept that part from you on purpose, knowing you'd want to leave after how they treated you. I take it you don't want anything to happen to the house?"

"No, it's all I have left of my family. I wouldn't expect you to understand but in Savannah, things are different. That house is alive, in a sense, and it's withstood everything from hurricanes to the Yankees. The spirits of my family still live there. I can't lose it. Now that I have discovered all this, I'm going to fight for it. I just have to be patient a little bit longer."

And try not to worry about the strange voice saying I wouldn't make it to my birthday or the violent attacks.

"That's good. You don't seem to be the kind of girl to back down from a fight. So, I'm guessing this is where the good news comes in?"

"Maybe. Mr. Bradley also told me my mama had set up a trust fund that I would have access to once I turned eighteen. A trust fund my stepmother knew nothing about, at least we assume that. He's calling now to make sure it's still there in its entirety. I wouldn't put it past her to have found out and taken it."

He studied me for a bit. "You're one of the strongest people I've ever met. It may sound corny but I felt it even when we first met. Maybe it was the way you shot me down or seeing you're normal after what I witnessed this morning at the set. You deserve a break."

Before I could say anything about his surprising observations, Martin came out of his office smiling and I stood.

"I talked to an associate at the bank and your trust fund is intact. We've agreed to add another layer of protection to the account. No one can access it now unless they have both of our signatures. Better safe than sorry, right?"

I let out a sigh of relief and hugged him. "Thank you so much. You have no idea what this means to me. I'll come back on my birthday and maybe we can get the papers filed to get Marietta out of my house."

"If we had more time, I'd suggest filing to become an emancipated minor but it would take too long and it would tip our hand to Marietta. Just remember what I said Quinn, be careful."

He had no idea how much I was going to take that advice to heart.

Chapter Nine

We said goodbye to Martin and walked out of the office. It felt as if there was a new spring in my step, as though a load had lifted off my shoulders and every other cheesy cliché that applied. It was nice to actually have an idea of what was going on in my life and how I might be able to come out of it.

"Now where?" Jason asked. "I'd suggest we go celebrate some place with air conditioning but I'm guessing you'd turn me down flat. How can you handle this heat? I'm melting."

I couldn't help but laugh. "I would absolutely turn you down. This doesn't make us BFFs. Sometimes it's easier to share things with a stranger. As far as the heat, you get used to it."

It was a brutally hot day. Not a lot of people were out and the ones who were sat listlessly on benches or front porches. Things in the South moved at a different pace.

"You're great for my ego, you know that?" He bumped me playfully with his shoulder.

"I'm sure you have no problems whatsoever with your ego."

I took a second to put a hold on the friendly feelings. Developing any kind of crush on him meant traveling down a dangerous road and I needed to avoid any one-sided emotional attachments. Before he could come back with something he considered witty or flirty, I continued talking.

"I texted Abby earlier and told her to meet us at Moon River Brewery, where her mama works. The owner lets us use it for investigations. It's supposedly one of the most haunted buildings in Savannah."

"Sweet, the most haunted building in the most haunted city. That should be interesting. So, why ghosts? Is it because you lost both of your parents so young?"

The last thing I wanted to say was 'because I can feel them' or bring up his dead brother, so I stuck with a general answer.

"In a sense, yes. You said it yourself, you can't be in a place like this and not at least wonder. Especially when you can almost feel it." Oops, almost too much.

Jason had a funny way of making me want to confide in him, which was something I had to be careful about. The thought of being hurt and my general lack of trust, made me work hard to keep him at a distance. It was turning out to be harder than I thought.

"I get it. I'm staying at one of those older hotels downtown. I hate new places. As crazy as it sounds there are times when I swear someone is in the room with me. Or I'll sense someone walking down the hall behind me. I've never experienced it before."

"That may be a residual haunting. It's energy trapped in a place that keeps repeating itself, like a song on repeat. They're not aware of you. To them, they're just going about their lives, the lives they think they're still a part of. That's what I love so much about old buildings or my house. Even when it's just me, I never feel alone." As hard as I tried, it was impossible not to get caught up in his enthusiasm.

"I'd love to see your place."

The idea of showing up at home with Jason Preston in tow made me equal parts giddy and terrified. They'd probably assume I put a spell on him. That's the only way he'd be with someone like me.

We turned the corner and I was saved from having to answer him.

Moon River Brewing loomed in front of us. The four-story building looked harmless from the outside. The pale stone exterior was made of common Savannah brick and the windows on the empty floors were clean and inviting. Still, something about it hinted at what went on inside. Or maybe that was only because I'd witnessed it.

"Let's go around back."

I led him into the alley. Abby's mom, Barb, worked as a waitress on the weekends and we knew all the kitchen staff. Abby and I had the run of the place most times and the manager assured us as long as we were careful and let him keep any evidence we found, we could go into the unoccupied floors of the building when no other groups wanted to use it for an investigation.

We found Abby sitting at a prep table in the kitchen waiting for us and I properly introduced her to Jason. No one else seemed recognize him, which was really starting to put a damper on my preconceived notion of him being an egomaniac; a notion I wanted to cling to.

After shaking his hand a little skeptically, Abby turned to me. "On a scale of one to ten, how bad was it?"

"Oh, about an eight or a nine. I'm sure I'll be in trouble whenever I do decide to go home so let's make the most of tonight. Jason wants to see what we do, so I thought what better place than this?"

I could tell she was dying to ask why I changed my mind about Jason so I ignored her questioning looks. ·

"Agreed. I already talked to Mr. Manager and we're good. Can we eat first? I'm starving."

I nodded as Jason went to sit at the prep table and we joined him after ordering sandwiches. Abby made no attempt to be subtle.

"So, Jason, what's life like in bright, shiny Hollywood?"

He turned his killer smile towards her. "I wouldn't describe it as bright and shiny. I've always thought of it as a black hole. It sucks you in and life as you knew it outside ceases to exist."

"Oh please, you're telling me that being a young, rich, hot actor isn't as wonderful as everyone imagines?" The words were out of my mouth before I could stop them.

Jason leaned close to me. "You think I'm hot?" I fixed him with my iciest glare, which didn't seem to work. "Fine, I'll take your silence as a yes. Fact is I'm never there. I consider Colorado, where I'm originally from, to be my home. When I'm in California I stay in Malibu to avoid the whole Hollywood scene. L.A. is a hard place to get used to."

Hearing him talk about Colorado reminded me of the story about his brother. That was the part of Jason that most interested me.

"Do you miss Colorado?" I asked.

"More than you can imagine. I'd never planned on getting into acting and tried out for Home on a whim. I never thought I'd get it. When I'm not working, I spend more time in Colorado than anywhere else. I miss the mountains, the crisp air in winter. Even the people, they don't have as much to prove."

Abby got a dreamy look on her face. "Winter...I wish I could experience an actual winter. Heck, I'd be happy with seeing the actual seasons change."

"I miss winter. We'd get snowstorms that dumped over a foot of snow at a time. It's one of the most beautiful things I've ever seen." He looked at me as he said the last part.

I fidgeted in my seat and was saved by one of the line cooks saying our sandwiches were done. While we ate, I brought up the subject of why we were there.

"Do you know anything at all about ghosts, Jason?"

"In what way? I mean, I've seen the TV shows so I'm fairly certain of

44

what an EVP is. Besides, last I heard ghosts were still a mystery. Unless you consider yourself an expert."

I wanted to call him a smart aleck but Abby saved me.

"Everyone kind of has their own ideas about spirits or ghosts which can actually affect how you see them. I think that's why it's always a woman in white or a little boy. Your mind sees something it doesn't recognize or feel comfortable with so it transfers it into something familiar. A spirit might not have enough energy to manifest into anything other than a mist or a ball of light or even a footstep."

"And you guys have documented spirits?"

"We have," I answered, "recorded some great ones in this building but we let the owners keep what we find. It's part of the deal. Mostly, the ghosts here haven't given us much trouble but there are rumors of some evil spirits as well. We try not to provoke or say anything that might anger them. Others do but I show them some respect."

"I agree with the idea of not upsetting them. Let's made sure we stick to that plan. Do you think we'll see anything tonight?"

"The chances are very high. We haven't had a night here where something didn't happen, even if it was just hearing footsteps or knocking. It's a very active place. You have to keep yourself open to the possibility and learn to be patient."

"Is it normal to have second thoughts about this?" Jason tried to joke but I heard a trace of nervousness in his voice. I couldn't help but tease him.

"A big tough actor scared of a little ghost? I knew you were all an act."

Abby laughed loudly while Jason fought to keep a grin off his face. He held up his hands in defense.

"I'm not afraid to admit it. I'll hide behind you, gladly sacrificing you to the legions of undead."

"My hero," I drawled sarcastically.

Chapter Ten

We finished eating and answering more of Jason's questions. His tension started to ease into curiosity and I got the feeling he was a little excited. We led him up to the second floor and began getting out the equipment.

"I brought along another camera, my personal digital, so we have more," Abby said as she pulled out a small pink camera. "Unfortunately, since you aren't familiar with what we're doing, this one's yours, Jason."

I watched him hesitantly take the pink camera then turned before he caught me grinning.

"As we go into rooms, take pictures," I explained, pulling out my big digital camera. "We've discovered part of it's based on feelings so let those guide you to where you point the camera. You said you knew what EVP's are right?"

"Electronic Voice Phenomenon, it's a voice you catch on a recorder you didn't hear with your own ears."

"Right, Abby and I both have digital recorders. You'll hear us asking questions to try to get a response. If you feel there's something you want to ask, go for it."

Abby launched into some history. "This building started out as the First City Hotel in 1821. Eleven years later, there was a murder downstairs and by 1864 the hotel ceased operations, probably because of the War. In 1999, the restaurant opened downstairs so most of this building is still in its original condition. They have tried to renovate but each time they start, activity also picks up. Workers will get knocked off ladders, objects move, and supposedly a woman was pushed down the stairs."

"Wow, okay."

He sounded nervous so I gave him an encouraging smile. "I wouldn't worry too much. We tend to stay out of the basement where the evil spirits are."

His eyes widened and he started fidgeting with the camera.

"Alright, I'm ready. Let's head all the way up first and then work our way down." Abby went up the first couple of steps and handed Jason a flashlight as she passed by.

We walked up to the top floor and wandered through the rooms. I found myself very self-conscious, not because of the building or why we were there but because of Jason.

Those forbidden thoughts stopped when Jason came to stand beside me. A loud crash sounded from the room on our right. I felt Jason jump and inch even closer to me.

"Hello?" Abby called out into the dark. "Is there someone here with us?"

All three of us were absolutely still, but no more sounds came from around us.

I asked, "If you're here, there's no need to be afraid. I think I heard you. If that was you, could you do it again?"

We'd turned off our flashlights so the only illumination was the light coming from outside and the narrow view we saw through the screens on our cameras. From our right I heard a scuff, like a shoe moving on a dirty floor. I saw Abby turn in the direction and begin filming.

Another, quieter bang came from behind us. It was the kind of stuff I was used to in this building, though I sensed Jason's tension growing by the minute. It surprised me how active it was already, surprised and pumped up. This was what I loved.

The darkness, the holding your body still to keep quiet and the unexplained noises would have scared normal people. Thank goodness, I wasn't one of them. It was a comfort knowing life continued in one form or another.

Abby walked farther along the hall, filming the area in front of her. Of all the floors, we were on the one that seemed the most consistently active. One more knock or bang came from the far end of the hall and Abby motioned she was heading that direction.

Jason was still glued to my side. If we hadn't been experiencing activity, I would have loved teasing him about it.

He smelled clean, a breath of sunshine and fresh air. I couldn't believe I was standing in the middle of a haunted building thinking about what he *smelled* like. It also dawned on me we were almost touching. It made my palms instantly sweat and I had to get a better grip on my camera. I started snapping pictures, forcing myself to concentrate on what I was there to do.

"Are you expecting company?" he whispered. When I didn't answer he continued, "Someone's coming up the stairs."

Turning my head slightly, I listened for a sound from the direction of the stairs. Sure enough, I heard slow footsteps. Occasionally the steps themselves creaked or groaned as if a person with actual weight were on them. The sounds were faint but obviously moving up towards us. .

My eyes adjusted to the dark. If something was there, I didn't want to startle it by turning on the flashlight. I moved slowly to the stairs using only my camera's LCD screen as illumination and waited.

I heard Jason follow. He started to say something but I elbowed him. He must have gotten the message because he shut up.

The air changed, growing heavier and heavier. People always say when something spooky happens, every hair on their body stands up and that's exactly what happens. It was similar to standing in the middle of a lightning storm. No other words did it justice.

I knew the feeling; it meant we weren't alone.

If anyone asked me, I'd freely admit I still experienced a small twinge of fear in situations like this. The expectation of the unknown and of what I might come face to face with never left me, regardless of my strange ability to communicate. Eventually the fear lessened but never fully dissipated. Evil entities did exist. I should know. I was living with one.

Jason stepped closer and I knew he'd sensed it too. I raised the camera and started snapping a quick series of shots in the direction of the staircase. It seemed that with each picture I took, the temperature of the air dropped. Soon, I saw the white vapor of our breath in the dark.

From being in the building before, I recognized this spirit. It was female and over time, I had come to learn certain things about her. She searched for her children who'd stayed here when the building was used as a hospital. An outbreak of fever had swept across the city and the dead piled up. Many people brought their children here to die. I wished more than ever that I could actually talk to the spirits. Seeing and sensing things about them wasn't enough anymore.

I wish I could help you, I thought.

So do I.

I jumped, which startled Jason beside me.

"Are you okay?" he whispered breathlessly.

"Did you say something, before?"

"No," his voice was in my ear so I knew he still stood very close. "All I've been able to hear is your camera and something else. Like something's moving around us."

I nodded, not really caring that he couldn't see me. The voice in my head

48

hadn't been me. It had tone and a heavier accent than mine. The only other time I'd heard a voice was with Marietta. Even though this one was different, the sensation of having another voice in my head felt unnatural. Normally, I was fine with whatever abilities I had. Feelings, hints and apparitions were much easier to deal with than voices inside my head.

Before I knew what I was doing, I'd cleared my head and thought '*hello*'.

This time nothing answered. Almost immediately, the air changed again, back to normal. It was easier to breathe and the static feeling disappeared.

I let out a breath I hadn't been aware of holding.

"What was that?" Jason's voice shook a little.

I flicked on the flashlight and turned it towards him. "That was a ghost, a spirit."

He came alive, almost bouncing in place. "Holy crap, that was crazy. The air changed somehow and I heard movement, like clothes rubbing when you walk. I thought a person was standing right in front of me. I knew if I reached out, I would have touched someone."

His excitement transferred onto me and I temporarily forgot about the voice I'd heard. "I know. That's how it is. You're lucky, not everyone can experience something their first time and we encountered one of the friendly ones. There are some nasty spirits in this building but they are a whole other experience."

"Did you get anything on your camera?"

"I'm not sure," I answered as I began going back through the pictures. "With the small screen on the camera, sometimes you don't notice anything until you can look at it on a monitor. Wait, here."

I gazed at the picture in the tiny screen. I'd caught some kind of mist, something not much lighter than the surrounding darkness. It had been standing right in front of me, exactly as I'd sensed. I showed it to Jason.

"Oh man, it's the shape of a person. It's hard to tell, though, it is so faint. It can't be that easy."

I narrowed my eyes as I said, "It's not that easy. You got lucky tonight. We haven't even been here thirty minutes."

"I'd bet everything that someone was standing right in front of us. Are you, what do they call it, one of those sensitives?"

That question brought up a whole mess of personal details I really didn't want to get into with him. I ignored the question instead and said, "Come on, let's find Abby and show her this."

Chapter Eleven

The rest of the night was uneventful but Jason still vibrated with adrenaline as we walked up Lincoln Street in the direction of my house. Luckily, because of the heat, there weren't many people out or I'm sure Jason's presence would have caused a stampede. I followed his lead and stuck to the shadows when we passed someone on the sidewalk.

It wasn't my idea for him to walk me home. I argued and even tried to lose him on the dark streets but he was crafty. He didn't let me out of his sight. The guy just didn't get the hint.

"I still can't believe what happened. I mean, I've always been kind of a skeptic but that was crazy."

"No matter how long or how many times you experience something paranormal, it's hard to get used to."

"Sounds as if you've experienced it a lot."

I wasn't sure what made me open up, maybe the hope that if I told him he'd go away. "When I was little mama used to tell me stories about Savannah and about the people who lived here before us, even those who were still here in a sense. She said it was a city built on the dead and populated by them as well. As a girl, I thought they were only stories. Some might think she had no right telling spooky stories to a young child but you know how it is here. You said you sensed it yourself, Savannah is different."

He nodded. "It's very different. Something about it feels so old and there's so much more here than what you see with your eyes. I thought it was my imagination but some of the crew from the movie mentioned the same thing. Now, after Moon River, I know."

"People chalk it up to the architecture, the trees, the many cemeteries right in the middle of town. Every single war fought on American soil had a battle here. In the Revolutionary War, tens of thousands of soldiers died and many were buried where they fell. It creates a mood and messes with your head. It makes you believe the stories. Anyway, as I got older, I started seeing things."

I paused and when he didn't say anything, I continued. "It started off as a flicker out of the corner of my eye, something there I couldn't quite focus on, or explain. As I got older, I sensed more information. I knew the man who went up and down the stairs at my place was a soldier and he gave me the feeling he still protected the house. Things like that. It's weird because the older I get, the more these skills, if that's what you call them, get stronger. I think I might even be able to hear them now, which is new."

Jason didn't say anything, which convinced me I had said too much. Maybe he was used to being the most interesting person in the room, or the street. Or maybe he was trying to come up with something witty to say and as usual, had a hard time with it. His silence made me nervous. Why didn't he say something?

"You asked. I'm a freak," I mumbled with deepening embarrassment.

Finally, he shot me the dimpled grin. "Honestly, I think it's kind of cool. You've gotten a glimpse into a world beyond ours. A lot of people would kill to have your ability. You shouldn't think it makes you a freak."

"Too bad that's not what people think when they look at me." I hadn't meant to say that aloud.

"Why? Because you dress that way? That's stereotyping. You and Abby did the same thing to me, thinking I'm a shallow Hollywood stud."

"I still think that, by the way."

"It's okay, I'm used to it. I'll surprise you when you least expect it. Besides, you want my professional opinion?" He paused, but not long enough for me to answer. "I think you dress like you do to avoid unwanted attention."

That bothered me. "I'm not trying to avoid anything and I don't exactly fade into the background. Besides, you're not a professional. And maybe I like wearing black. What do you know anyway?" I was babbling.

"Don't get me wrong, I'm not saying there's anything wrong with how you dress. The whole 'goth' thing works for you. Your hair and your coloring, it makes you stand out even more. Not all guys are into the cookie-cutter Barbie type."

"Yeah right, you don't have to flatter me. I can tell you right now I'm not the squealing and worshipping kind of girl."

"I've noticed," he mumbled before changing the subject. "So, have you ever seen your parents or sensed them, whatever it is you do?"

"No, and I've tried so hard. Both my parents loved this city and they loved our house. Things haven't been the greatest since they left. I've always assumed there'd be some kind of contact with them, but I've had nothing."

He stepped a little closer as we walked. "Do you think it would help if you could see them?"

Just then, I remembered his brother. Thinking I could help Jason contact him was the only reason I stayed in Jason's company. At least that's what I told myself.

I had to rethink my answer with his loss in mind.

"I honestly don't know. We're not supposed to understand death. Whether the people who stay behind do it because they want to or because it's not their decision, we might never know. I won't deny I'd love to have the opportunity to ask Daddy what he saw in my stepmother and why he thought I'd be safe with her. Maybe there are some things we're not meant to find answers to."

"It would be nice to understand why some people die and some live."

He sounded so sad and I wished there was more I could say to him. I couldn't imagine having been in an accident and watching a sibling die. It struck me then how similar we were. I wouldn't say it made me happy but I felt we understood each other in a way others couldn't.

Jason was talking again. "So why did you invite me with you, to the lawyer's office? I mean, apparently I annoy you but you let me tag along."

That was harder to answer. I still wasn't entirely sure why I'd let him come. It was like my subconscious battled my conscious and convinced me he wasn't as bad as I wanted to believe. My seesaw attitude confused not only him but me as well.

"Good question. I'm just hoping I don't regret it one day." I gave him a flippant answer wanting to stick to the unimpressed side of my head. Luckily, we reached our destination. "This is my block."

York Street intersected Lincoln right near Columbia Square. Our house sat on a trust lot, one of the smaller lots surrounding the old squares scattered throughout Savannah and part of the city's original design. All the historic homes in the area were made of 'Savannah grays,' the brick common to the area. With the exception of the house built behind mine, the others dated back to before the War.

Jason gazed down the street. "Wow, nice neighborhood. Which one is yours?"

I pointed. "Halfway down on the other side of the street. I don't want to get any closer. I'd rather not have to explain you to Marietta."

"Okay, but someday you're going to have to tell me about this family of yours. Um, what are you doing tomorrow?"

For the first time, I didn't doubt he actually wanted to see me again. I watched as he fidgeted, shuffling his feet and clearing his throat. Gone was the cocky actor I forced myself to see. Replacing it was a guy who acted very nervous about my answer.

I didn't trust him yet but he intrigued me enough to want to see him again. Plus I wanted to see if my initial instincts were right in sharing some personal stuff with him.

"It all depends on how much trouble I'm in for the incident earlier with Marietta." I handed him my phone. "Put in your number and email address. Don't put it under Jason, put it under Dr. Sherman or something."

"Dr. Sherman?" He grinned and handed me his phone to do the same thing, "Where did that come from?"

"Well, doctor because it's not suspicious and Sherman because any true Southerner in their right mind will shy away from the name Sherman."

It took him a minute to get it. "Oh, right, the burning of the South after the Civil War."

"Actually, it's the War of Northern Aggression," I said in my heaviest drawl.

He laughed and handed me back my phone. "Fine, I'll remember that. I'll be in touch tomorrow morning to see if you're on lockdown or not. I love your accent by the way."

"Alright, bye." I waved, embarrassed by his compliment, and ambled up the walk. As I opened the front door I fought the urge to look back at Jason and to run from the house. Marietta would probably be waiting up for me.

Chapter Twelve

The minute I walked into the house, I felt it. The air was wrong, malevolent somehow. Once I fought past the fear, I recognized it as Marietta, or more correctly, the darkness taking her over.

I swallowed hard and forced myself to walk into the front living room, where it was strongest. The lights were out but I could still see the shadows pulsing and shifting, almost as if they were alive. Not even the streetlights made a dent in the air slithering near me.

My breathing sped up and I tried to search for the other spirits in the house, George and the soldier, even the strange one that appeared around me at times. I felt nothing.

"Welcome home, Quinn."

I squealed and jumped. From what I could tell in the dark, the voice came from the couch. What worried me the most was it sounded like Marietta, but underneath her voice something sinister echoed and my body shivered in response. I feared for my life but couldn't make myself move.

As my eyes adjusted to the dark, I once again became overwhelmed with the putrid smell of the river. It made me gag.

"I – I'm sorry, I lost track of time. I'm sorry about my behavior earlier, too. I shouldn't have disrespected you that way."

She barked out a cold laugh. "You're a Roberts through and through. It's sad to see what we've become."

"I don't understand." She didn't make any sense but I tried to concentrate and take advantage of the opportunity to learn something.

"Of course you don't. You have no idea what our family is capable of."

"What do you mean 'our family'? Who are you?"

54

"A Roberts daughter, like you, left to fend for herself. They valued their name and their precious house above everything, including me."

Before I could ask anything else, it all changed. Marietta shook her head and looked around, unsure how she'd gotten to the couch. There were black circles under her eyes, giving her a hollowed out appearance. It was a far cry from the high maintenance woman I was used to.

"Quinn? When did you get home?" Her voice sounded tired but normal. The room warmed with the glow of the streetlights and the shadow retreated into the background.

I couldn't stop shaking. My knees threatened to dissolve into nothing at any moment.

"A few seconds ago, Marietta. I'm sorry I took longer than I should have. And I was way out of line earlier."

Marietta pinched the bridge of her nose between her fingers, as though she had a headache. "Don't speak to me that way ever again. Go to bed. The girls and I will be going to Atlanta in the morning. I'll leave a list of things for you to do on the kitchen counter."

I hurried out of the room and up the stairs before she changed her mind. I was terrified and left all the lights on in the attic, as I'd been doing every night lately. I felt George in the corner, hiding, and knew I should offer him some encouraging words, but I didn't have any in me. Who would comfort me?

It affected me more than I thought to see Marietta so vulnerable. I knew the shadow entity had to be feeding off her and I wondered how long it'd been going on. Kicking off my shoes, I lay on the bed and thought back to when I first met her.

When Daddy first brought her home, she'd been uptight and snotty but not in an evil way. She'd acted exactly how I envisioned a rich Atlanta housewife to act, nothing more. In the year before Daddy died, we'd even come to an uneasy friendship and it made me hope one day it would be more.

It wasn't until after Daddy died that she started to change. Four months after the funeral, I saw the shadow entity for the first time and experienced the mean nature of its influence. I didn't think it was a coincidence that when Marietta's entity showed up, so did the one who fought back for me.

Ever since the night I'd almost been strangled things had stayed disturbingly quiet, until tonight. Even if all it did was speak, I felt the power throbbing off Marietta. Whatever that thing was, it seemed to be waiting. It almost killed me the last time and what might happen next terrified me. I thought about what she said and why she had such a hatred for my family.

Catherine. It had to be Catherine.

No matter how much I wanted to get away from Marietta and the twins, I couldn't leave them now. This thing hurt me and it could just as easily hurt them. I needed to figure out what she wanted and how to stop her. I had to be strong.

Sleep was a long time coming. I literally had the urge to sleep with one eye open but eventually I drifted off. Right as I went completely under, I felt the protective spirit beside the bed.

The last thing I remember was the feel of a hand brushing the hair from my cheek.

Chapter Thirteen

Surprisingly, I woke up the next morning feeling great. Marietta and the twins would be gone the entire day and I'd be able to do anything I wanted. I got up once they were gone and sped through the list of chores left for me.

It had been such a long time since I had something to look forward to that I didn't even mind cleaning the disgusting bathroom I shared with the twins. I knew they were filthy on purpose and no matter how much I tried to keep it clean, it didn't work. Normally, the globs of hair and spilled lotion and used tampons would send me into fits of rage where I imagined delivering all kinds of bodily harm to them.

Not today. Today I tried to ignore it, along with the crippling doubt that Jason would even be in touch.

Stepping out of the shower, I heard my phone chime with a new text message. The message was from Dr. Sherman and read, "U free or locked in the basement?"

I smirked and typed, "It's usually the attic but I'm free. Step monsters gone all day. Come over." Before I changed my mind, I hit 'send'.

He mentioned wanting to see the house. Logic told me that since Marietta wasn't home, it would be safe. The last thing I wanted was for something here to cause him harm. He had found a way to work himself into my life, something I still wasn't sure I wanted. I did enjoy talking to him, once I got past the jangled nerves. No, that wasn't even true anymore. I liked him, which annoyed the heck out of me, but I figured I might as well let it play out. He'd be bored soon enough and on to more challenging pursuits.

"On my way," he replied.

I dried my hair and dressed in khaki shorts and a black tank top. I ran around straightening up an already pristine house and realized I really was nervous. Not even Abby had been in the house recently and now, Jason Preston would be here. What was I thinking? He couldn't come here.

Before I could text him back to change where we met, the doorbell rang.

"Here we go," I muttered.

Taking a deep breath, I opened the door. He stood there grinning at me. I saw a car pull away from the house and a large man across the street, near the square, trying to blend in. He must have been one of Jason's bodyguards.

"Morning, Quinn."

"Hi." I stood there with the door open for what felt like forever. "Oh, come in. I'll give you a tour then we can leave. I need to go to the library."

"Okay." He entered the house and scanned the room. "I wasn't sure if we'd be going anywhere so I brought my disguise."

Jason pulled a baseball cap out of his back shorts pocket and pulled it on. Then he slipped on a pair of wire rimmed glasses. I laughed. It didn't do much to take away from the fact that he was incredibly attractive but someone glancing at him might not be able to tell it was Jason Preston.

"What're you laughing at? It's a good disguise and it works, most of the time."

"Okay, if you say so. I see you also brought your muscle, Mr. Important." I jerked my chin in the direction of the street.

He grinned again and pulled off the glasses. "It's hard to sneak away from them. The studio thinks it's necessary for some reason. Most of the time, I don't even notice them. This place is much bigger than I thought last night. How old is it?"

I felt self conscious as he entered the large foyer with the enormous sweeping staircase. The focal point was the giant antique brass chandelier hanging from the two-story entry. Portraits of my ancestors graced the walls although not as many as there used to be. Marietta claimed they frightened her. Following Jason, I ran my hand lovingly over the banister.

When I was a little girl I loved playing dress up and walking as elegantly as I could down the stairs, pretending to be Scarlett O'Hara. Or I'd dream of descending them to meet a boy who stood nervously in the foyer with Daddy. They reminded me of another girl; a girl who still had her place among the oldest families in town, a girl on the verge of becoming a woman whose dreams come true, a girl who would raise her own children in this house. Maybe now those dreams could come true after learning the truth about the will.

It was a dangerous road to go down so instead I told Jason about the house.

"Old. It was built in 1831 and has survived the years pretty much intact. At one point, it was supposedly the finest house in all of Savannah. The grounds took up the entire block. There are sixteen rooms, not including the attic. No one's really done any major remodeling apart from updating the kitchen and bathrooms and the electricity. Air conditioning was added, of course. Every generation did its part in keeping the house in pristine condition."

I led him into the front parlor, ignoring the couch Marietta sat on last night. It still gave me the creeps thinking about the foreign voice coming from her mouth.

"This is the front parlor, or I guess it's more of a living room now. All the floors are the original hardwood. Marietta hates the upkeep on this place. She's always complaining but I look at it as a labor of love. That door leads into the formal dining room. This way," I led him back through another door, "is the kitchen."

"Wow, awesome kitchen."

I smiled. Marietta updated it not long after moving in and I agreed it was a great room. The large windows let in plenty of light and the dark cabinets and granite countertops gleamed. It was the kind of room that shouldn't work in an old house, but it did. There was also another large fireplace original to the home.

"I wasn't expecting to see stainless steel appliances. Don't old houses like this have to be historically correct?"

"You've done your homework," I said and ran my hand over the counter, "but no. This house is listed on the National Historic Register but most of the rules only apply to the outside. They make allowances for updated interiors as long as the exterior is maintained in the original condition and as close to the original handwork as possible."

"Did you memorize that?"

I felt myself blush. "Well, I love this house and up until the last couple years, it has been in the Historic Homes Tour. I used to love dressing up in period gowns and showing people the house. It's one of our silly traditions. This house is all that's left of my family. I can't explain it."

"People down here are real sentimental about their houses," Jason said. "It reminds me of the one we're using for the movie. It might even be a bit older. I can't remember the name of the house now. They all have names here, I've discovered. Anyway, the owner follows the crew around like a man possessed. They can't set the equipment there or they can't move that piece of antique furniture. I think the director's ready to strangle him."

"Luckily, Daddy was never that obsessed. He let me be a child in here, running from room to room, sliding down the banister, even climbing on things I shouldn't have. I knew other kids who also lived in historic homes who weren't allowed to do anything. Their bedrooms were full of centuries old furniture and they were only allowed to play in the servant's quarters, which weren't as well refurbished. You have to let kids be kids."

"My parents were that way, too." A sad shadow crossed over his eyes. "They were the kind who totally overdid the holidays. Our house always looked like Santa threw up on it."

"I know what you mean. This place turned into a winter wonderland only without the snow." I sighed and stared out the window. "It's been five years since Daddy died and I haven't had a Christmas since. Marietta and the girls put up a tree but they go to Atlanta so I'm left alone. Abby and her mama invite me over but I hate imposing. I think I miss holidays the most, and birthdays. It might sound selfish but my best memories are of us as a family at Christmas. It's such a magical time."

Jason didn't say anything but I could feel his heavy, pitying stare. I hoped he would forget what I said. I hated sounding so 'poor me' all the time. I pointed out the rounded window overlooking the backyard and hoped the house would distract him.

"I told you the house originally took up the entire trust lot. A trust lot is the four smaller lots surrounding one of the town squares. They were once considered places of privilege. Now we only have the carriage house, or basically the garage, a shed and another small outbuilding at the back of the property that I think was used for either storage or slave quarters."

"The carriage house is huge."

I studied the building that captured his attention. The carriage house was almost as big as the main house. The brick was not in as good a shape as the main house and I noticed one of the rounded doorways had begun to sag. I couldn't remember the last time I had gone up to the second floor but when I had, it was huge, empty and dusty.

"Well, when you consider it used to house the carriages and the horses that pulled them, it needed to be big. The carriage driver or stable hand would have lived in the rooms above. I read that it once housed close to a dozen horses for the Roberts' many different carriages. The people who built the house on the other side fought to get it torn down because it sits too close to them. We won that, thankfully. The second floor has great light and I've already started dreaming about putting my photography studio and darkroom up there."

I felt him watching me for a while before I turned to him. "What?"

"You come alive when you talk about this house. Now that I see you here, I can't picture you anywhere else. I don't blame you for fighting to keep this place. Any other plans?"

"Maybe a pool." I grinned and gazed back at the window. "A lot of historic homes have added them so I don't think it would be a problem. Other than that, I'll concentrate on making it the home I remember. It has been neglected too much. Let's go upstairs, I'll show you the bedrooms."

After I showed him the three bedrooms and office on the second floor he looked at me questioningly.

"You're staring again." I eyed him close.

"So, where's your room? Call me crazy, but I assumed it wasn't one of those cotton candy pink disasters. You don't strike me as a frilly bedroom kind of girl."

"That's because I'm not." I wrinkled my nose at him. "I wouldn't be caught dead in a pink bedroom. It would make me physically ill. What's your bedroom like? Mirrors on the ceiling, oversized pictures of yourself on the walls?"

Leaning close, Jason asked, "You've thought about my bedroom?"

My breath caught in my throat at his proximity. He was close enough that I saw specks of brown in his eyes. Nothing could stop the blush I felt working its way across my face. All my strength went into playing it cool.

"*You wish*. You want to see my room? Fine. Follow me."

Even with my back to him, I sensed the big smile on his face and became aware of how my own lips wanted to curl up traitorously. I stopped at the door to the attic, opened it and pointed upward.

Chapter Fourteen

"No." He peered up and then back at me. "You're kidding."

"I wish, but now that I've worked on it a little bit, I kind of like it up here."
I led him upward.

The stairs opened up in the middle of the huge space. To the left was everything I had yet to get to, boxes, trunks and armoires full of hundreds of years of junk. My living area was to the right and the only outside light came from the two tiny windows at either end. A ceiling fan circled lazily up in the rafters, moving the heavy air. My portable air conditioner barely made a dent in the heat, even on good days, and most of the time I didn't even mind the bugs.

"Originally, the entire space was one large pile of junk. All you see to the left is stuff I haven't had a chance to go through yet. It's not as bad as it looks. Sure, I have to share a downstairs bathroom with the disgusting twins but I savor my privacy. And it's been awesome going through all this history." I directed him over to my antique desk. "Here's a good example."

Jason studied the letters. "Roberts? These are about your ancestors?"

"Yeah, and look at this one." I pulled the one about Catherine to the top. "It's from Catherine Roberts to a William Jennings. She mentions their upcoming marriage and thanks him for helping her family out. Ten months after their wedding, she died of mysterious circumstances. In fact, they never found her body. I think Jennings helped out the family and she was the payment."

"Ouch, I can't imagine that went over very well but people were used to arranged marriages back then. Did you find anything more about her disappearance?"

I sat on the bed as I sighed and explained. "No, not really. Catherine went from being a prominent member of Savannah society to never attending

62

functions. She no longer served on committees and only appeared with her husband a handful of times. A couple of these letters mention Jennings, who was a Yankee and not very well respected. He was a suspect in her disappearance and harassed her family after she disappeared. He wanted the house desperately from what I understood of the other letters.

"There's a newspaper clipping below those. Yeah, that one. It says Jennings disappeared not too long after the letters were written. No one ever saw him again. Then, at the end, in a related note it says Margaret Roberts had a breakdown. I'm sure I'm not the only one who thought it was a pretty convenient coincidence."

He read the article and didn't say anything for a minute. "Even if what you're saying is true, if the Roberts family had something to do with Jennings' disappearance, what does it matter now? It sounds like a great mystery and, I don't mean to sound rude here, but why spend your time on this? So what?"

Here's where it got tricky. Could I trust him not to think I'd lost my marbles? Most people would laugh at my conclusions and suspicions. I had already told him way too much. What the heck, if he left and never came back it would probably be for the best solution for both of us. I closed my eyes and blew out a slow breath.

"I need you to keep an open mind, please. It's quite possible you might leave this house when I'm finished and never look back."

He came over and sat beside me on the bed. "I'm a pretty tough guy. I don't run away from things."

I believed him. "I've told you how there have always been strange things happening in the house, spirits and all that." He nodded. "Well, ever since Daddy died there's been a different presence here and it seems to have attached itself to my stepmother. It's hard to describe. A dark shadow has tried to take her over and her shadow is no longer her own. It moves and pulses on its own power.

"I think it's what affects her behavior. Sometimes she's her normal nasty, rude, and demeaning self, and I can live with it. Other times she's vicious, cruel, threatening. Those times, it's as if the shadow or darkness or whatever it is grows, changes the air, and expands out. The other morning I was in the kitchen with her and all the cabinet doors and drawers slammed open and closed. She didn't even flinch. Last night, she spoke to me in a voice that wasn't quite hers. She told me I was a true Roberts and I had no clue what my family was capable of."

Jason took my hand and I realized my entire body was trembling.

"Coming from anyone else, I'd think you were full of crap. But after what happened last night and being around you, I believe you're telling the truth.

Who knows, maybe you'll still find a rational explanation for all this."

Relief blossomed in me. Until then I'd fully expected him to say I'd lost my mind.

"That's not even the worst of it," I added. "A few days ago, in Marietta's salon, it reached out to me somehow. I felt its presence again. And it said I wouldn't see my eighteenth birthday, which is a couple weeks away. Then, the same night I found those letters, I laid here afterwards wondering about what really happened. I'm not even sure what it was exactly but the last thought I had was about Catherine and wondering whatever happened to her.

"Suddenly, a weight pushed me down on the bed. Cold fingers surrounded my neck. I couldn't breathe, or move. I came so close to dying and I remember accepting it, maybe even welcoming it. But then a light exploded in the room. For a second I got a look at the thing and then it was gone. I still don't know what to think but it was the same thing attached to Marietta. I recognized it. And I'm fairly certain it's Catherine."

Jason stood and took a few steps. "You've got to be kidding me, Quinn. You're saying something in this house threatened you and then tried to kill you? And you're still here?" He turned back to me. "Are you crazy?"

"Where can I go, Jason? I have no money of my own yet and I'm still a minor for a couple more weeks. You can't imagine how much I've thought about this. I only have to put up with this a little while longer, and then I'll get my trust fund. The problem is now I'm worried about what'll happen to Marietta and her daughters. I don't want them hurt."

He sat back down on the bed, closer this time and grabbed my arms. "From everything you've told me, it's only getting worse and you might not have time. If you're as serious as I think you are, this entity wants something from you. It's not going away."

"I think it might be after some kind of revenge."

"What do you mean? Did you do something to one of her ghost friends?" I appreciated his dry humor. Some of my tension melted away even as I realized he might not actually be joking.

"Nothing as simple as that. I believe it's Catherine. If Jennings helped the Roberts family with the intention of marrying into the fabled Southern lifestyle, Catherine was an innocent pawn. Maybe she was abused and it resulted in her death so she wants revenge against her family. It's the only reason I can think of that accounts for her disappearing from the public eye. What if she was sent into a horrible situation?"

"True, being forced into a marriage, especially an abusive one, would have changed anyone. Even more so if it ended in her death at the hands of her husband. She might be angry enough to take revenge on the last Roberts. You."

All I could do was nod. I wasn't even sure if it was true, but it made a strange kind of sense. Her vicious attitude towards our family made sense now. Killing me seemed a little extreme but, like Jason said, maybe it changed her in the worst imaginable way.

I looked at him as the implications sunk in. Until now, I hadn't been able to come up with a tangible reason for her threats. So much of the puzzle was still missing. I needed to figure the rest of it out. In order to do that, I needed to keep a low profile.

Jason studied my face and leaned in closer. I wondered if he would kiss me but before he did, he jumped.

"Something moved over by the desk." He sounded scared and after the stories I'd been telling, I didn't blame him.

I'd been so distracted by Catherine and Jason and wondering if he was going to kiss me, I didn't notice George leaning near the desk. I looked at him in my peripheral and saw him studying Jason closely.

It almost made me laugh. Right when I thought I'd shared every strange thing about myself, something else popped up.

"Don't worry. Remember I told you there were other spirits in the house, peaceful spirits?" He jerked his head up and down in quick movements. Then it occurred to me. "You can see him?"

"Yeah," Jason whispered. "Not if I look at him straight on but from the corner of my eye I see a little black boy with bare feet. What the heck is going on, Quinn?"

I laid my hand on his shoulder. "Ever since I was a little girl, I've called him George. He's a good spirit, Jason. You don't need to be afraid of him. George, this is my friend Jason."

Jason let out a crazed laugh. "You talk to him?" His voice rose to a higher pitch.

"You have to imagine being a nine year old girl. Talking to a little boy I saw would have felt normal. I guess I kept doing it out of habit. He can't talk back but he understands me."

Eventually, Jason seemed to relax a little. "I–I don't know what to do. I mean, does he just hang out?"

George smiled which made me do the same. "Sometimes he does. I haven't seen him since the night I was attacked. He disappeared before it happened."

I noticed George flicker and a feeling of helplessness crashed through me. I turned my attention to him. "It's okay George. You wouldn't have been able to do anything to help. I'm glad you came back though."

"You don't think he was the one who made that thing go away?"

George shook his head sadly.

"No, whatever saved me was powerful. For the life of me I can't come up with any theories about what the light was. I'm stumped."

We were both quiet for a long time and I sensed George getting weaker. Eventually, he faded away completely.

Jason let out a relieved sigh. "Wow."

"I'm happy you could see him. I think he did it on purpose to show you I wasn't alone here."

"You're one interesting girl, Quinn Roberts."

I grinned. "You say that like it's a bad thing."

He returned the smile cautiously. "It's not a bad thing. Maybe intriguing would be a better word than interesting. I'm filming a movie about the paranormal, about vampires, and here I am in the middle of a real life paranormal experience." He wiped a hand over his face. "Give me a chance to catch up."

"Okay, let's get out of here. I think you've had enough of my house for one day."

He stood and followed me down the attic stairs. "Good idea. Where are we off to?"

"I need to do some more research. I understand if you wanted to go do something different or more glamorous." I almost hoped he would jump at the chance.

"Are you kidding? You're not alone anymore Quinn. I want to help you figure this out. Maybe George thinks I can help. I'll warn you though, if you keep giving me crap about being all 'Hollywood'," he made quotation marks with his hands, "I'll come right back with an 'I see dead people' joke."

I laughed loudly at him and it felt good to let go. Before I answered him, I locked the house as we left and took a deep breath of the fragrant air.

"Fine, no more Hollywood remarks but I can't have you squealing like a girl again because I'm thinking this is only going to get more unreasonable and scarier the farther we go with it."

"Awesome," Jason muttered.

Chapter Fifteen

We spent most of the day at the historical society and same as before, there were only mentions in the society columns and newspaper about Catherine's strange absence from events.

"Wow, this place is awesome," Jason said as he studied a brittle copy of an old newspaper. "Is it still standing?"

I leaned over to see. He pointed to a faded black and white photo of the long torn down Pulaski House. Once, it was the finest hotel of its time, which always amazed me, considering it had been owned by Yankees. The hotel, known for its lavish parties, was too lavish for some Southerners to resist.

"It has been torn down for a long time but was supposedly haunted. I heard even the building that replaced it has reports of the same kind of paranormal activity. That is one place I would love to investigate."

"You and your ghosts." He smiled and shook his head. "What caught my eye was that it talks about Catherine being at these parties, at least until she married. The most notable thing after that is Catherine not being in attendance. They mentioned it a lot. Her absence was noted by the papers as well as the patrons. Then, after a few months, they stopped printing anything about her at all. At least until they found her body. I kind of get the feeling she was the 'it' girl of her time."

Jason surprised me. He threw himself into the research, claiming it was exciting. I guess it would be if I didn't have the nagging feeling my life was in danger. And he was good at the research. He could skim an article or page and pick out anything interesting. Must have been a habit he picked up from reading all those scripts.

We also found an older article hinting about her impending engagement to the son of a wealthy landowner. All that did was add more speculation to the fire. I tried not to be discouraged even though I related to a soldier going off to war and not understanding my enemy.

Jason and I left the historical society building with his bodyguard conveniently blending in as a normal tourist and walked downtown to the riverfront where we found a small seafood restaurant that wasn't too busy. After we sat down and ordered, Jason brought up our fruitless search.

"I don't think digging up the past is turning out to be very productive. Maybe you need to look at this from another angle."

"Well, I hope you have ideas because I'm all out." I sipped my sweet iced tea.

"I might have a few." I liked him better in his 'disguise'. It made him more approachable, in a sense, even though the girl in the corner booth kept eyeing him. He continued, "What if it's a form of possession? Try looking at it from a paranormal standpoint. I'm sure there are plenty of others doing the same thing as you and Abby. You should find people with more experience to help you with this."

I thought about that for a bit. It actually made sense. I wasn't the only one who'd ever had a nasty encounter with an evil entity. Someone else might have some ideas on how to deal with it, especially if it was a possession. I'd been thinking more along the lines of a haunting and possession hadn't yet entered my mind.

It would be nice to have a knowledgeable person tell me if it was something I could fix.

"That's a good idea. I hadn't thought of that. I'll get Abby on it. She spends a lot of time at Moon River Brewing now that she's working there part time. Quite a few paranormal groups come through there. See, you're good for something."

I texted Abby as the waiter delivered our food.

"So, how come you're free today?" Jason asked.

"My stepmother and stepsisters are in Atlanta, probably looking for pageant stuff or costumes for your masquerade ball."

He winced. "I forgot about that. The ball is this weekend, isn't it? I thought it was a lame idea but the studio heads wanted to do it as a 'thank you' to the city for allowing us to film. I'm really not looking forward to it."

"I hate to break it to ya, but you're in the wrong business if you don't enjoy dressing fancy and sucking up to people. Most of an actor's job is publicity."

"I realize that, it just makes me feel more like a piece of meat than I already do." He looked embarrassed and pushed his food around on the plate. "I'm aware of how ungrateful I sound, too."

"Nah, you're right. You've still got a couple years before you become a true self-centered celebrity."

"I hope not. Please tell me you're going to come to the ball. I need someone there to keep me grounded. Think of all the people we can make fun of."

I stared at him, wide-eyed as we stood up to leave. Had he just asked me to go with him? Or was he only wondering if I'd be there?

"Probably not a good idea. Have fun though." Any dreams of going to a stupid ball with Jason were dangerous, not because Marietta and the twins would be there but because of my growing feelings towards him. I wasn't an idiot. I knew that when the movie wound up production, he would leave. I didn't need to be doing anything crazy such as going on a pretend date.

Jason grabbed my arm as I walked away. "Why isn't it a good idea? Why do you hide from things?"

I shook my head at him. "You don't know anything about me."

"Then give me a chance to."

"I want to, Jason, I do. In the last twenty-four hours you've learned more about me than anyone in my life, except Abby. The only way I've stayed sane was by not letting anyone get close. I take care of myself first and don't trust people. It doesn't matter that I feel a connection to you. Can you understand why I at least want to keep my distance from you and not be another notch in your belt?"

I didn't realize I'd spoken so long or so passionately until I saw his eyes staring intensely at me.

Then, he spoke. "You're stereotyping again. I do understand that you're only trying to protect yourself and that you've done it out of necessity. You want the truth? I think you're awesome. It might come across as a line, but I've never met anyone like you. All the girls I meet are exactly the same; vapid, self-centered and boring. I look at you and I see the kind of girl I *want* to know, even when you're rude and sarcastic. Which adds to it somehow."

My glare slipped and I wanted to believe him but I steeled myself to say. "Nice try. You're not going to flatter the pants off me."

He didn't react as I had expected. "See! That's what I'm talking about."

I couldn't help the small grin forcing its way through.

"You're quick and witty and wounded…"

"Wait, wounded? Is that how you see me?" I interrupted him. "I'm not some sad puppy for you to save, Jason. If that's what you want go find Little Miss Perfect Blonde and save her from an unfortunate tanning accident. You're wasting your time here."

That ticked him off. "Come on Quinn, that's not what I was saying. I'm not trying to save you because you don't need it. You're brave and strong and fighting for something. You've had a crappy life since your dad died but there's still warmth in you. I can see it no matter how hard you try to keep it hidden. The snarky exterior is mostly show. I know it and so do you. You just have to decide how it affects the relationships in your life, even possible relationships. Think about it. I'll call you later. Count on it."

Before I could respond, he was gone.

I wasn't entirely sure what happened just now but it left me feeling a mixture of curiosity and restlessness. Jason's words thawed a part of me I either forgot about or didn't know existed. I didn't see what he found so impressive about me but I kind of wanted to find out. He knew exactly what to say to hold my attention and turned out to be nothing as I expected, or hoped. I needed to learn to let myself go.

I heard a loud noise and saw a bus pulling into the stop half a block ahead of me. Running forward, I boarded it without a second thought. My destination was Bonaventure Cemetery, where my parents laid in eternal slumber together. Today would have been Daddy's birthday and I couldn't avoid it any longer.

Chapter Sixteen

My mind wandered on the ride out and I almost changed my mind when I transferred buses. It had been over a year since I'd visited my parents' graves. I never spent much time wondering why I spaced my visits so far between. Maybe it had to do with the reminder of how much I missed them.

I got off the bus with a group of tourists and followed them through the entrance.

Bonaventure Cemetery was located on the site of the Bonaventure Plantation. The original plantation house was built in 1762, but after both houses were destroyed, it was now used mainly as a cemetery and historic site.

This cemetery stood out in sharp contrast to the much older Colonial Park cemetery, where we met Jason. Colonial Park had a dark, almost sinister feel to it. The trees were old and gnarled, the flowers only bloomed at night and even the tombstones were corroded. It felt the way an old, scary cemetery should.

But Bonaventure was beautiful and sat on a bluff looking out over the Wilmington River. Flowers perfumed the air and many of the plots were landscaped to resemble little parks. Savannahians made coming to visit their ancestors an event. That included park benches and fresh flowers around the graves to make the visits more comfortable.

I've heard people say that we were similar to the Japanese in how we worshiped our ancestors. Each generation paid homage and gave respect to those who came before them. It was one of the truest ways to describe how we felt about our past.

So many people used the phrase 'the past is alive' to describe a place. Here, in Savannah, it was the truth.

Most of the older generations of the Roberts family lay buried in Colonial Park, but it had been closed to new burials for a long time. Now, our family plot was here. I made the mental note to see if I could find Catherine's grave next time I went to Colonial Park. It might be a good thing to have on standby.

I made my way down the shaded paths and eventually reached our plot. As much as I was able to block the feelings from the spirits populating the cemetery, some still got through. Places like this, where the dead were higher in number, tested the mental walls I'd constructed to keep them out of my head. There were too many to ignore.

The lush, green grass invited me to sit down and as I settled into place I tried to fight the rush of emotion. I hated crying here. The last thing I wanted my parents to see, if they were still here, was my sadness and weakness.

"Hi Mama," I whispered. "Happy Birthday, Daddy."

Pausing, I opened up my mind and sorted through the barrage of information coming from the spirits nearby. None of them were my parents, so I locked it back down.

I sighed.

"It doesn't matter how many times I try, I always expect to feel one of you. The only thing I can do is hope you're together in a better place."

A tear slipped from my eye and I brushed it away impatiently.

"I really need your help right now, Daddy. All this stuff about the will and the bank and the house, none of it makes sense. I need someone to reassure me that what I'm fighting for is worth it and that I'm doing the right thing."

The wind caressing the trees came as my only answer.

"And Mama, I met a guy. He's an actor, which I'm sure you and Daddy would be hesitant about. Jason sees me in a way not a lot of people care to. I find myself wanting to tell him everything about myself, and it's scary. He said all these nice things to me but I'm so scared to take the chance and open myself up to him with everything else that's going on."

I sat there for a while longer enjoying the stillness. Then, something prickled the back of my neck causing the hair to stand up. Turning, I saw Marietta with a handful of flowers. The moment we locked eyes, her face went vacant and I sensed the dark presence loom out of her.

"Don't worry Quinn, soon you'll be lying here with them forever." The voice came from Marietta but her mouth did not move. Her hand lifted and she pointed behind me.

I looked back and my skin went cold.

In the empty space beside Mama and Daddy's tombstones, was one that hadn't been there a moment before. I took a couple jerky steps forward until the name on the stone froze me in place.

Quinn Roberts.

As if in a trance, I reached forward fully expecting my hand to pass through the pale granite but it didn't. My hand lay on the cold stone. I whipped my head back to Marietta.

"What is this?"

Laughter. Then the voice said, "This is your future."

The ground opened up beneath me and swallowed me up. I landed with a thud at the bottom of an empty grave. The top of the six-foot high walls were just out of my reach. There was no way out. In a panic, I turned in circles, fruitlessly searching for an exit. Marietta walked to the edge and looked down at me with those dull, lifeless eyes. The shadow whirled around her, obscuring her face at times, and stirring up the now familiar river scent.

I was terrified but before I even had a chance to scream out for help, the walls of the grave began falling inward. I was being buried alive. A constant flood of dirt and rock rained down on me, filling the space at an impossibly fast pace. I clawed at the walls trying to get out, not caring that my fingernails were being ripped out by the compact earth. I knew the cemetery at this time of day held dozens maybe hundreds of people but my desperate cries for help went unanswered.

The dirt crept higher; locking me in a vise there was no escaping from. It reached my neck but my body still fought. The one arm, still free, stretched feebly for the clear blue sky above me. In the midst of my cries and gulping sobs I heard cold laughter. When the first clumps of dirt fell in my mouth I didn't taste it. I tasted death. I felt the dirt slipping down my throat and blocking out the disappearing air. Then, it covered my eyes and the light vanished. The entire thing lasted less than a minute, not even giving me a chance to accept defeat. But as the darkness settled so did despair.

My lungs screamed for air. The pain of it was the worst thing I'd ever experienced. It felt like a lifetime, but in reality, only a couple seconds passed before a comforting sense of calm pushed into every inch of me.

This wasn't how it was supposed to end. I never got a chance to say goodbye or even a chance to fight. I wanted to fight.

The moment I thought those words, there was a sucking sensation and I felt the pressure surrounding me lessen. Suddenly, I could breathe again. When I opened my eyes I saw I was kneeling in the grass next to my parents' graves. I turned my head and noticed Marietta still standing there, vacant eyes and all.

Chills raced through me as the reality of what I experienced sunk in. Catherine showed me I was far from safe and I understood she was playing with me. I hung my head in an attempt to catch my breath and shot to my feet after catching a glimpse of my arms.

I was covered in dirt. It clung to me everywhere. Panicked, I brushed at my clothes and my arms, trying to get it off me. But it wouldn't go away no

73

matter how hard I wiped at it.

"What is happening?" I yelled. It was then I realized Marietta was gone. The only people I saw were an elderly couple who hurried by when they saw me. I wondered if they saw the dirt or if all they saw was a crazy girl swatting at her arms and talking to air.

An irrational fear seized me. The cemetery no longer felt safe. I needed to get out of there. A crazy laugh bubbled up inside of me. I had just been buried alive and I was afraid of a bright, sunny open space? It didn't seem right.

I remember rushing out of the cemetery, of being on the bus, and the freakish stares of the other passengers. The dirt still wouldn't come off and the logical part of my brain told me there was no way it was real. It had to be an illusion. But the odd looks I received made me doubt that.

When I got home, I rushed in and accidentally slammed the door.

I heard voices in the kitchen and as badly as I wanted to get upstairs and look in a mirror, I was drawn in their direction.

The twins and Marietta gathered around the breakfast bar eating a pizza. I almost didn't recognize Marietta. She laughed and smiled with the girls, looking more like herself than she had in five years.

I stood there in shock watching them and longing to be a part of it, even as I was wary of the change in my stepmother.

All three of them caught sight of me at the same time. Their expressions ranged from concern to disgust and to amusement.

"Are you okay?" Anna asked.

Suzie shot her a dirty look and said, "Of course she is. Where have you been Quinn? Bathing with the other cows?"

I caught my reflection in the stainless steel fridge and all the blood drained from my head. Clutching the cabinet, I couldn't believe what I saw. I was covered in dirt, exactly as I feared. How was it even possible?

I shook my head in denial at the image in front of me. I didn't understand.

"Quinn, where were you?" Marietta demanded.

Something about her question snapped me out of my daze. "I was at the cemetery. Today was Daddy's birthday."

Marietta wiped her mouth daintily and gave me a sad smile. "I know. I meant to make it down there today but I got caught up in work. I'll go tomorrow."

My brows drew together in confusion. "But I saw you. You were there. I talked to you."

She stood up and brought her glass to the sink. "You must have fallen down and hit your head. I wasn't at the cemetery today."

Chapter Seventeen

The next day life returned to normal. I stood at my family's beck and call every hour of the day. The up and down emotions of the last couple days wore me out and reality came crashing in with a vengeance.

Whenever Marietta talked down to me or ordered me to do some menial task, I wanted to confront her about what happened at the cemetery or what I'd found out about Daddy's will. It took every last bit of strength for me not to come clean. Instead, I focused on the outcome I wanted, being rid of Catherine and having Marietta out of my house.

Sleeping the night before was impossible. Every time I closed my eyes I felt the suffocating pressure of the dirt on me. Lately, all my nightmares had been the kind you have when wide awake.

I met Abby downtown on one of my ridiculous errands for a quick bite at an outdoor cafe. We hadn't had a chance to talk much lately and naturally, she was full of questions about Jason and Marietta. I made the decision not to tell her about the day before. It wasn't because I didn't trust her because I did, more than anyone.

The problem was I'd always been the type of person who fought her battles on her own.

"So, how's it going with Mr. Hollywood?"

"It's not," I grumbled. "He's texted me a few times but we kind of had an argument."

Abby's eyes widened. "What did you argue about?"

"He thinks I'm wounded and interesting, blah, blah. He doesn't know anything about me."

"Are you blind? You think a guy like him would waste his time if he wasn't interested?"

She wasn't exactly making it easy to ignore my feelings. I wanted to hang out with him. All I had to do was to convince myself to take that risk. A couple weeks with Jason were better than none at all.

I shrugged halfheartedly. "You're right. I'm just facing the inevitable fact he's only here for a couple months. I don't see it going anywhere but that doesn't mean I can't take it one day at a time for now."

Otherwise, we talked about less frightening things, such as Marietta and how life would change once I had the house to myself. Living alone in that huge house sounded intimidating but I'd deal with it when that day came. Maybe if Abby stayed in Savannah for college she could move in with me.

Walking out of the café I heard an all too familiar voice to our left.

Sure enough, Anna and Suzie were coming towards us. My stomach sunk in anticipation of what I knew was sure to come.

"They really need to take better care of who they allow in this part of town. We can't have you two scaring off the tourists." Suzie greeted in an overly sweet way.

Abby stepped right up and got in Suzie's face. "Careful, sweetie, you wouldn't want to make me mad."

I saw Suzie's eyes widen in fear. I suspected that they'd put so much effort into spreading the lies about us being witches or Satanists that they almost believed it themselves. Of course, the strange events happening at home didn't help our cause.

Fully expecting Suzie and Anna to walk away, I watched in shock as Suzie reached up and yanked on Abby's hair. Abby cried out in surprise.

"Did you really just pull my hair?" She laughed in disbelief but I also heard how ticked off she was. "Just because you got away with this stuff in high school doesn't mean we won't stick up for ourselves now."

Anna snorted. "And you think that's going to scare us? When are you going to understand you don't belong anywhere? All you had in school was each other and nothing has changed."

"Because you two are freaks." Suzie was still in Abby's face. "That's all anyone will ever see when they look at you. Both of you are sad and pathetic little witches."

"But Quinn is your sister, your family. Does that not compute?"

"She is *not* family. She's just someone we got stuck with."

Abby pushed her away hard and I looked over at Anna, waiting for her to join in. A confrontation like this was four years in the making but it wasn't something I wanted to happen.

Reluctantly I slipped between Abby and Suzie, who were ready to rip into each other.

76

"Come on guys, this is stupid." I frowned at Abby. "And you of all people should realize it is so not worth it."

I watched as Abby took a deep breath and slowly relaxed. She looked Suzie up and down. "Yeah, you're right. Let's go."

We walked away without a second glance. I half expected them to come after us but a block later, I looked back and saw that they hadn't.

"Quinn, those girls are first class she-cats. You should have let me pummel her."

"While I agree it would have been satisfying, if only for a few minutes, I would've paid for it when I got home."

"I know. I didn't stop to think about that. Maybe the day after your birthday, after you've given them the papers kicking them out, I'll let them have what they deserve."

"Sure," I laughed. "Or we could take pleasure in knowing that they're homeless."

She thought about that for awhile. "Okay, you're right. That'll be enough for me."

Later that night, I waited for the twins to bring up the incident with Abby but to my surprise, they didn't. Anna watched me carefully. It wasn't a threatening look, more as if she was trying to really figure me out. Maybe my actions today, stopping Abby from going off on her and her sister made her think there was more to me than she thought.

I almost giggled at the thought. Thankfully, I was distracted by a door slamming upstairs. The girls squealed and Marietta stared at me with the same eerie concentration she always did.

That night I knew something was going to happen. It might have been the look from Marietta or the confrontation with Anna and Suzie earlier, but I braced myself for anything. I waited for hours, trying to keep my eyes open.

Eventually, I fell into a deep, peaceful sleep.

I woke up to the sound of clomping steps early the next morning.

In a haunted house, you hear footsteps all the time and eventually it becomes just another sound. These were different. They were heels and the steps didn't sound very graceful.

Curiosity won out over the normal need to stay away from my family and as I walked down the stairs from the attic, I found the source of the noise.

Anna was walking up and down the hardwood floors of the hallway in high heels. I imagined she was practicing for the pageant but I might have sworn someone dropped ants down her pants. She kept one hand on her hip, which twitched back and forth in a very uncomfortable way. It always surprised me how someone tall, blonde and beautiful could be so clumsy. Anna was always tripping over nothing but because she was popular, everyone thought of it as 'cute.'

I tried to sneak away without her seeing me. Now that I knew who it was, I didn't want her to catch me but she saw me turning to leave.

"Oh, it's just you Quinn," she paused before continuing quietly. "Did you see me walking? Do you think it looks horrible? It feels horrible."

"Why do you care what I think?" I couldn't help it. Any time Anna or her sister were nice to me, I got wary.

She must have heard the suspicion in my voice. "I'm only asking because Mom and Suzanna are gone and I have a feeling you'll tell me the honest truth."

Well, Anna was right about that. I sighed and walked back down the few stairs to stand in the doorway.

"It woke me up and I thought the house was coming down. I don't know anything about pageants, but I can't imagine they'd think you're beautiful and graceful while you clomp across the stage."

She actually pouted, sticking her bottom lip out. "I know. I just can't do it."

Unsure what came over me, I said, "Show me again."

Surprised, Anna gathered herself up and walked towards me. I guess walking was a relative term because it wasn't what she was doing. I wasn't sure if it was the heels that made her body take on such an odd angle or what. Her head and shoulders stuck out way ahead of the rest of her.

The floor and the walls vibrated from the impact of her shoes. I fought against laughing. It was reassuring that some people can't have everything.

When she finished she looked at me expectantly.

"I think you need to keep your shoulders back and your spine straight. You're ready to launch forward. And try not to walk so heavy."

She tried it again and I was surprised to see her posture actually looked better. Still, she clomped like a horse.

"Better. You're still making too much noise so try not putting your foot down so hard."

Again, she couldn't master it and stomped her foot in anger childishly.

"I can't get it. Here," she bent over and pulled off the heels, "you show me."

Part of me thought it was a trick but the other part, the part that hungered for family, reached out and took the shoes.

I didn't have much practice in heels myself so it took me a couple of tries to get the feel of them. Finally, I was able to walk with just a slight click-clack, the sound a high heel normally gives off.

Anna looked impressed and shocked at the same time. "How do you do that?"

"I guess when you try to be invisible you learn to walk softly to draw less attention to yourself." I shrugged and handed the shoes back to her.

She studied me for a long while and I held my breath, waiting for the apology about the way they'd treated me all these years. Instead, she put the shoes back on and walked quietly down the hall. Looking back at me, she smiled but that was it.

I was halfway back up to my room when I heard a quiet 'thank you' follow me up the stairs. It didn't make me feel happy or satisfied. It made me feel sad. Years of subjection to their abuse, spurred on by their mother, was too much. The reason for their hatred was always right out of my grasp.

Was it because I was so close to Daddy before he died? He'd been their fourth stepfather. Marietta had never given them the opportunity to get close to a father figure. Or was it because of my ability to shrug off caring what people thought? I imagined the upkeep on their perfect, popular lives was exhausting. I had a certain amount of freedom being the outcast. I felt comfortable in my skin regardless of how I closed myself off.

It didn't matter what their reason was, it would have been nice to have a sister, or two.

Chapter Eighteen

Over the next few days, the only contact I had with Jason remained via text and random phone calls. When I saw his name on the screen of my phone, my heart wanted to leap. It took a lot of work to keep it grounded.

Several times, he asked to see me but I just couldn't bring myself to do it. After admitting to Abby that I would give it a chance, part of me held back. Plus, I was embarrassed by how I reacted to him the other day. I needed to concentrate on staying one step ahead of Marietta and Catherine. Now was not the time to be worrying about boys.

But I couldn't help it, especially when he asked me again to go with him to the ball. Even thinking of saying yes made me fear for my life. If I defied Marietta in that way, who knew what would happen.

"What's for dinner?"

Marietta brought me back to reality by coming into the kitchen followed by Anna and Suzie. I snapped out of my thoughts. Suddenly, my hands felt too big and I had to concentrate on not dropping anything.

"I made spaghetti, the way you like it with the meat sauce, and salad and garlic bread. You guys can go ahead and have a seat. I'll serve you."

We made it through dinner and I was thankful to escape upstairs with my food. I passed the soldier on the stairs and had a sense of him stepping aside and nodding to me as I passed. He was so different from George because he never made any attempt to communicate with me. I got the feeling he was there for a reason and hoped that one day he'd explain what it was.

The house felt alive tonight. The weight of the entire place was pressing down on me. George was waiting in my room and it was obvious something was bothering him.

"Hey, George." I sat down and dug into my food. "Something feels different tonight."

He moved over beside me and I took another look at him. He wasn't as transparent as usual.

Danger.

The minute I heard the child's voice, I knew it came from George. It was the first time I had ever heard his voice or had any sense of communication with him. This must be important.

"What danger, George?"

His eyes grew big and I noted how they were rimmed with long black eyelashes.

Danger, you must leave.

I felt the fear and sorrow throbbing off him. A lump lodged in my throat. "I can't leave. What would happen to the house, to you, if I leave? I can't turn my back on all of you and my family's legacy."

You might die.

I wanted to pull him into my arms and offer some kind of comfort. I knew my life was threatened but I truly believed the outcome was worth the risk. It wasn't only my life at stake; Marietta's was, too.

"I understand the risks and am okay with them. Please don't worry about it." Talking about the danger scared me more than I would ever admit aloud. The concern coming from this sweet little ghost boy threatened my resolve. Then I thought of something.

"What's your name? I know it's not George."

I don't remember.

I leaned closer and looked into his beautiful black eyes. "I promise when this is all over, we'll find out together."

He didn't believe me but I knew he wanted to with as much longing as a spirit could possess. From what I'd witnessed, longing seemed to be one of the strongest emotions spirits were left with.

Right as I was about to curl up with a book, my cell rang. It was Jason.

"I swear I had a perfectly good excuse for calling but I forgot." I heard voices and shouts behind him so I knew he was on the set, taking time out of a movie to call me, of all people. "How've you been?"

"Good. It's been a pretty quiet day, actually." *Considering that I was almost buried alive yesterday,* I added silently. "Sounds busy there."

"It is. Tonight I get to test out my fighting skills and get tossed around with superhuman strength all while wearing a wire harness that'll help me move like a vampire. Did I mention the harness is very dangerous and uncomfortable to places I am desperate to keep? Did I also mention I kind of miss you?"

The mixture of warmth and irritation that hit me was confusing.

Jason cleared his throat. "I want to see you again. Is it okay to say that?"

"Don't say it any louder in case your adoring fans hear it." I sighed. "I don't know. There's so much going on right now. But I'm sure I'll have some time in the next day or two." The words surprised me because I hadn't meant to say them.

"Good, we'll figure something out. I'll be thinking of you tomorrow night. And I'll watch for you in case you change your mind about coming."

I didn't even realize I was smiling until after I'd ended the call. Jason had a way of sneaking up on me, of getting under my skin before I had a chance to stop it. He was so darn persistent. With him, I could live in the fantasy world that Mama always talked about. I could believe in her happy endings. Except I needed to make sure I remembered which was the reality and which was the fantasy.

My head was full of dreams when I fell asleep.

Hours later, an unknown sensation woke me up. I opened my eyes and knew instantly something wasn't right. It was too dark.

I sat up in bed cautiously and surveyed the area.

By the time my investigation made it to the right side of my bed, I'd almost convinced myself that I was imagining things.

Until I came face to face with Marietta.

I barely made out her figure in the darkness. She stood two feet from the side of the bed, her intense stare locked on me. I scooted as far away from her as I could and switched on my bedside lamp.

Shadows played across her face, painting her with pure evil. The shadow I had started thinking of as Catherine was there as well but it bounced and flowed like a normal shadow.

Marietta remained there, still as a stone, for a long time. The lack of any life in her body scared me almost more than the look in her eyes. They were boring into my very soul.

"Marietta," I squeaked out her name quietly, hoping it didn't anger her.

Nothing.

The longer it went on, the more I felt my body react. I started shaking and couldn't stop. It pulled me into that zone where you couldn't make a rational thought. As crazy as it sounded, I thought her stare would be what killed me.

Her eyes were full of hate but beyond that she was empty, nothing. Marietta was gone. Only her body remained. She was an empty shell.

All of the other times I'd had interactions with her and Catherine it had been a physical thing. This was different. This was an assault on my soul.

And it was working.

I lay in the bed curled up in as small a ball as possible. Even with my eyes closed, I felt the weight of her stare. I honestly felt as if I was going to lose my mind.

Then, I sensed her move. I opened my eyes and watched as she turned and walked away. The vacant stare never left her face, even as she walked out of the room.

I could breathe again but wasn't able to uncurl from the protective ball. I stayed that way all night, my mind focused on one thing, whether or not she would return.

I would not allow myself to fall asleep again.

Chapter Nineteen

Marietta and the twins spent the entire day getting ready for the ball. I mostly tried to stay out of their way.

I kept thinking about what Jason said the other day about being scared. I knew there was some truth in it. I'd spent so much time keeping my head down I was uncertain how to reach out and grab something I really wanted. I couldn't even stand up for myself without fearing some kind of fallout. That had to change.

It tempted me more than I ever thought it would, to defy everything and meet him at the ball. Screw the consequences, whatever happened would at least have happened because I took a chance. But even with my pep talk, I couldn't make myself get up and actually do it. If all else, at least I'd have a quiet night in the house to do research.

My lack of motivation didn't stop me from longing to be one of those girls primping all day, vibrating with the anticipation of what the night would bring. Since meeting Jason, I saw so many possibilities and so many things I'd missed. I wanted a life.

I was sitting in the kitchen eating when they came down. I knew they were supposed to be dressed as Southern belles but it was hard to tell with the layers and layers of lace and satin. The materials were beautiful and I truly thought if they had merely gone with the 'less is more' mindset, they would have shined.

Marietta's dress was a melon orange color, complimenting her pale blond hair and accenting the lack of color in her cheeks. I hadn't noticed until then how pale and drawn she looked. She was starting to look more and more affected by the entity holed up inside her. As far as the presence attached to her, it felt excited, almost bubbling with energy.

One more thing to convince me it was female.

Suzie and Anna wore similar styles of dress with laughingly full hoop skirts. Suzie's was a light blue and Anna's a soft yellow.

"Don't wait up," Suzie sneered cruelly.

As they gathered up their stuff, the doorbell rang.

"Quinn, get that," Marietta bit out.

I moved past them and opened the door, even though Anna stood only a couple feet away.

The man wore a normal tux, not the kind of thing I would have pictured someone going to this ball to wear. I didn't recognize him and assumed he was someone escorting my family to the event. Over his shoulder I saw a long black limousine parked at the curb.

"Can I help you?" I asked.

He smiled, "I'm here to escort a Quinn Roberts to the Savannah Heritage Ball."

My jaw dropped as Marietta stormed up and pushed me out of the way. Jason. He must have done this. It was a nice gesture but he should have known better.

"What did you say?" Her anger simmered below the surface and I braced myself as the shadow loomed behind her.

His smile fell into a look of confusion. "I was told to pick up Quinn Roberts from this address and drive her to the resort. Do I have the wrong house?"

"Who ordered that?" Suzie roared.

"I don't have that information, miss."

Marietta glared at me. "You have the right location but Miss Roberts will not be attending the ball tonight. I'm afraid it will just be my daughters and I. You can take them out to the car and I'll be right along."

The man opened his mouth to argue with her but she shot him a look that made him take a couple steps back. "Of course, ma'am, I'll be waiting outside."

In spite of the twins' questions, Marietta shoved them out the door without a word. They had a hard time fitting through the doorway with those huge hoop skirts. It would have been funny if I wasn't nervous about Marietta. She slammed the door and turned to me.

Prepared to have her unleash her wrath one me, I was surprised when she smiled sweetly. "I suppose you're not going to explain?"

I shook my head. "I don't have any idea, Marietta. I swear. I haven't made any plans to go tonight. I know my place."

Of course she didn't believe me. She grabbed me by my hair and dragged me up the stairs. It brought tears to my eyes and I fought not to cry out. "I don't know what you're up to but I don't like it. Whatever you planned for tonight isn't going to happen. It's my night! I haven't been to a ball in so long, since before the War. Tonight, I'll be the one they look at, the way it used to be."

We reached the door to the attic and Marietta threw me forward. I caught myself on the steps and whirled to face her. She looked like Marietta, but the shadow throbbed around her.

"Catherine?" I whispered.

She laughed and slammed the door in my face. I heard the lock click and the beat of her heels as she walked away. I turned to walk up the stairs and stopped at the sound of something heavy being dragged across the floor towards the door, which shook as it was pushed up against it. I guessed she moved a heavy piece of furniture to block the door, in case I figured out how to unlock it.

I knew she was gone because the house grew still and quiet in a way it hadn't been the last few days. Outside, the twilight darkened, matching my mood perfectly. I tried to reflect on what happened but all I felt was shock.

In the far corner of the attic, a faint light blinked and grew bigger and brighter. I felt the air change and instantly I knew this presence was the strange force that protected me. Sitting up on the bed, I watched the light pulse and move closer. I wasn't nervous. Something told me no harm would come from this energy.

Then, it changed and the light formed into the shape of a person. After a quick flash it dimmed, leaving behind a surprisingly solid woman.

I stared at her in shock. I was able to look at her straight on. Her image did not waver or flicker. Her clothing appeared to have come from the War era. The cut of her rose colored dress and the hang of her skirt resembled the antebellum costumes seen all over the city. It was what the twins' dresses should have looked like.

"Hello, Quinn." She spoke in a soft, breathy voice.

Apparently, I'd finally lost my mind.

The woman smiled. "Don't be afraid, dear. You've felt me before and I've been waiting until you needed me most."

"You're the one who scared off whatever almost killed me? And all those other times too?" I finally found my voice. Over the years, I had experienced many crazy things but this really topped it all. "Who are you?"

"I'm your great-great-great-grandmother, Margaret Roberts."

I gasped. "I don't understand. Why are you here?"

Margaret walked over and sat next to me on the bed. A thousand chills ran through me when I actually felt the bed shift under her, as if someone with actual weight and substance sat down instead.

"I have a story to tell you, Quinn and then I'm going to help you go to your young man. You've had too much tragedy in your life. It's about time we changed that."

I laughed at her. "You're going to help me see Jason tonight? What, you're my Fairy Godmother?" Her face remained blank as if she had no clue what I was talking about. "Fairy Godmother, from Cinderella? It's a story about a girl who – she's locked up and – oh, never mind." I ran my hands over my face. Maybe I was the only one who saw the similarities.

"You're an odd girl." She studied me closely. "I know you've been investigating the events surrounding my daughter's death and that of her husband. Would you like to hear what really happened?"

"Of course, I'd love to find out what it has to do with this house and if I really am in danger like she says."

Margaret nodded and took a deep breath preparing for the story she was going to tell. I settled in to listen to her voice, as slow and richly southern as Sorghum molasses.

Chapter Twenty

"After the War, most of the Roberts family businesses were broke. We poured everything we had into a losing cause. Our family watched and waited with all of Savannah's great families for their loved ones to return. And when Sherman marched into the city, he spared it. Everything changed after that. Our slaves went free and Yankees poured into Savannah looking to capitalize on our misfortune. Even in a city ravaged by war and newfound poverty, this house stood as one of the finest.

"Our family had dealings with a man named William Jennings. He was a Yankee. We borrowed money from him to keep our remaining businesses open and the opportunity to rebuild our cotton empire. You may have already gathered that William was not a good man. After about a year, he told my husband and me that he would be willing to forgive our debt in exchange for the house.

"Instead of our beloved family home, James, my husband, offered him something much more valuable to a Yankee; our daughter's hand in marriage. To a man like William, the opportunity to marry into one of the oldest families in Georgia was too much to turn down. We could have avoided all of this if it had not been for James' pride.

"You have to understand it was a tragic time. All our friends and neighbors were falling from their lofty heights, losing everything. The only reason we were still in business was because of Mr. Jennings. I understand the reason, but I'll never forgive myself for standing by and allowing it to happen."

Margaret smiled sadly. "Catherine was a headstrong girl and desperately loved her place in the social tiers of Savannah. She was so beautiful and vibrant. Many eligible bachelors chased after her and fought for her hand, but she only had eyes for one, Jackson Merriwether. The Merriwethers were one of the richest families in Georgia, probably in the entire South. Jackson was their oldest and a dashing young man. He came and called on Catherine many times and there was much speculation that they would wed.

"Then, the war happened. Jackson enlisted and vowed to return in a few months as a war hero. All those boys who enlisted thought they were going to be back soon. The pride of the South." She shook her head. "For years, he only managed to get a few letters through and she saw him once for about an hour near the holidays. Their love never diminished. Even after Gettysburg when he was listed as missing or dead, she clung to the hope that he would still come home.

"The day we told her she was to be married to a stranger I saw hate in her heart. She fought against it, but those were different times. She had to do what her father wished and she never forgave us. A couple days before the wedding she even tried running away but James brought her back kicking and screaming. They were married in a quiet ceremony and for the entire ten months they were married, I only saw her once. We corresponded but I always got the sense from her letters that she was being guarded.

"Back then Savannah was still a small city so it was odd to not have seen her at social events. From what I could tell, William was a controlling man with a vicious temper. I heard rumors and gossip about him beating her and other unspeakable acts. Each time I tried to call on her William told me she was ill. I should have done more.

"Around the time she died, Jackson came home. It was a miracle and my heart broke for them because by then it was too late. If only he had made it home a few months earlier, things would have been so much different for all of us. He went to see her but I don't know what happened because two days later she died. It destroyed Jackson. He left for the West and never came back.

"No matter how bad things were for her, they must have taken a nasty turn after the visit from Jackson. Maybe William caught her trying to leave. I'll never fully understand what happened to my daughter and maybe that's why I'm stuck here, to search for Catherine and beg for her forgiveness. We gave her to that horrible man. We sent her to a life of hell. We killed her."

She was quiet for awhile and I was at a loss for words. I knew how it hurt to lose someone you loved, but I doubted our pain was similar. I had a million questions running through my head but before I could ask any, Margaret continued.

"After Catherine's death, William became even more persistent. He'd wanted the house before but found satisfaction by marrying Catherine instead. I figured he was a man accustomed to having the best and not being denied. Once Catherine was buried, he took up campaigning for the house again. His offers and interest in the house became more and more outrageous. He was not a sane man. The amount of money he offered would have been indecent, even in your time. My husband didn't take his increasing threats seriously. I think he was too numb from Catherine's death.

"One day William came to the house. He was belligerent and demanded that we give him what was rightfully his. He felt that as the widower of a Roberts daughter, he should get the house. He was convinced we burned him on the deal because his wife died so soon. Clearly, he was mad.

"I don't need to mention all that was said but William and my husband began fighting and struggling. William had his hands locked around James' throat and said he'd beat the life out of him just as he had Catherine before he dumped her in the river. I don't remember much of what happened next. We were in the front parlor and I was standing next to the fireplace. I picked up the fire poker and struck him in the head. Even after he had fallen, I kept hitting him until I couldn't lift my arms again.

"My husband buried William out in the garden and I don't remember anything after that day. I died in a sanatorium, surrounded by darkness and nightmares, haunted by the memory of my daughter and what I did to her and Jennings. Catherine is the spirit haunting this house. She wants revenge against her family and you're the last one. I'm afraid she wants to hurt you to ensure our family name dies with you. All because of me."

It took a few minutes for everything she said to sink in. I felt scandalized by the fact she, of all people, had murdered William in this house but it wasn't as shocking as why Catherine wanted to end my life. Somehow, realizing that didn't scare me as I thought it would. It was a relief to finally know what and who, I was dealing with and why.

"I guessed most of that or at least sensed it. The obvious question in all this is how do I stop it? Can she be stopped?"

Margaret shook her head sadly. "I'm at a loss as much as you. Right now, she has a willing host who she is able to use freely. If she were simply a spirit as I am, she would not have been able to assault you but having a human host gives her power. She wants the life she was denied. Even more, she wants any Roberts to suffer as much as she did."

No matter what, I still wanted no harm to come to Marietta but separating Catherine from Marietta's body was going to be impossible.

The silence dragged on. I really didn't have any clue what to say to Margaret. Under normal circumstances, I would have had a million questions for her but right now, my predicament felt overwhelming. It had been a long, weird day.

One question popped into my head and I asked, "Is Jackson here, in this house? Is he the soldier I sense?"

She nodded. "He was destroyed after Catherine died and I think those strong emotional ties to her and our family are why he is here. He doesn't talk much."

"No, he doesn't. He's one of the more mysterious spirits."

"He is different than the young man I remember." Margaret stood and turned towards me. "However, I think right now, we should concentrate on getting you to the dance. The rest can be put on hold for one night."

"How are we going to do that? I'm locked in this room. Unless you have a pumpkin that will turn into a carriage, I have no way of getting there."

Confusion crossed her face and I almost laughed.

"Pumpkins that turn into carriages? I have no clue what you're going on about but the door isn't locked anymore."

I didn't believe her so I jumped up and ran down to the door. Sure enough, it door opened and nothing blocked its way. I slowly walked back up to her.

"How did you do that?"

"It doesn't matter. Now, from what I recall we must find you an appropriate dress. I think I have just the thing."

She walked over to an armoire in the messy part of the attic and opened it. I expected to see old, moth eaten clothes but instead there were five gorgeous dresses hanging with an assortment of undergarments.

I walked up behind her, immediately drawn to a deep purple gown, trimmed in lace and pearls.

"I think this one is perfect," Margaret said, reaching in and pulling it out, along with a corset and a hoop skirt. "We need all this if you're going to have the right effect."

"How can you touch things?" I'd learned a lot about spirits in the last couple of years and I knew it took a tremendous amount of energy for her to do what she was doing.

"How can you believe in ghosts and not in magic? It's sad, sweetie. All girls and young women should believe in the promise of magic." Unsure how to respond, I turned my attention back to the dress. "Maybe after tonight you will."

Margaret handed me the clothes. Luckily, like any good Southern girl, I knew how to put on the corset and hoop skirt. She came up behind me and tightened the corset to an almost uncomfortable state.

Before I pulled the dress on, Margaret studied me closely. "We really should get rid of those awful purple stripes in your hair."

I flashed an embarrassed smile. "They are extensions, I can take them out."

She looked relieved. "Good and make sure you curl your hair. I can pin it up when you're done."

Almost an hour later I was dressed and ready to go. Most of my hair was piled on top of my head and I didn't recognize myself in the mirror.

I didn't even resemble the poor girl who lived in the attic. In this moment I was the lady of the house, one who had opportunities and a full social calendar. The dark purple satin of the dress accented my dark hair and with the makeup, my face glowed. Thanks to the corset, my already small waist was tiny, standing out in stark contrast to the wide hoop skirt. The corset also did wonders for my chest, pushing up my cleavage high enough to entice any man with a pulse. It made me blush which only made it worse.

I couldn't deny I looked like a Roberts, though.

Margaret walked over and studied my reflection.

"Beautiful. I have one more surprise for you." She held up a dainty gold necklace. The pendant was in the shape of a teardrop. A dark purple stone surrounded by fancy gold filigree detailing took up the center of the drop. "This was given to me, when I was a young girl, on the eve of my wedding. I gave it to Catherine on the eve of her wedding, hoping it would somehow bring happiness to such a solemn day. William had it in his pocket the day I killed him. It was meant to be an heirloom. Maybe now it can be."

She placed the exquisite piece around my neck and fastened it. I don't know how else to explain it - it belonged there.

Tears pricked my eyes as I turned to Margaret. "I can ever begin to thank you for this."

She put an icy cold hand on my cheek. "You don't have to thank me. We're family, darlin'. This is what we do for each other. I wanted you to have a night to remember before you faced whatever is coming with Catherine."

I sniffed and nodded. "Have you dreamed up any transportation for me?"

"Of course, it's waiting outside."

She walked me to the door and my breath caught in my throat.

A horse drawn carriage sat out in the street waiting for me.

"It's perfect." I kissed her cheek, vaguely wondering in the back of my mind what the driver saw as I did this.

Carefully, I walked down to the waiting carriage, hoop skirt swaying side to side like a cloth church bell.

"Good evening miss." The burly driver took my hand and helped me in.

"Thank you. Do you mind my asking how you knew to be here?"

He gave me a strange look then pulled out a cell phone. "This thing rang and I picked it up, followed the directions."

I nodded with a wry smirk. The spirit world was full of surprises.

Chapter Twenty-One

The carriage pulled up in front of Savannah Shores Resort and Golf Course and I officially started to get nervous. The Mardi-gras type mask Margaret gave me felt heavy on my face but I loved the idea of no one knowing who I was. It felt safer.

After the driver helped me out, I walked to the entrance trying to appear much more confident than I really was. I handed my invitation to the lady at the door, another one of Margaret's mysteries, and followed the crowd of people inside.

It really was a sight to behold. I'd literally stepped back in time.

Gleaming marble floors reflected the dancers as well as a gold and crystal antique chandelier hanging over the center of the room. All the French doors on the far side of the room were open to the night, letting in the fragrant air. Candlelight danced along the walls from brass sconces.

The women were all dressed similar to me, true Southern belles, and the men were dashing as Confederate soldiers or wearing a suit and tails. A small orchestra played from the corner of the room and I saw an ice sculpture surrounded by large white Magnolia blooms and punch bowls. Magic shimmered in the air. Not the magic I witnessed with Margaret but the kind that made dreams come true.

This was another world; one I'd dreamed of being a part of and now I was.

As I walked farther into the room I got the uncomfortable feeling that everyone was staring. Sure enough, when I gazed around, I noticed many glances in my direction. Thankfully, I looked nothing like Quinn Roberts or else I would've turned and run away as fast as I could. I was fairly certain no one would recognize me.

I kept an eye out for Marietta and the twins, though. I didn't want to test my theory of being unrecognizable with them. More than anything, I wanted to find Jason.

About halfway into the crowded ballroom, I saw him. He wasn't wearing a mask but he looked dashing decked out in a very authentic looking Confederate soldier uniform. The mere sight of him made my palms sweat.

He raised his head and searched the crowd, watching for someone in particular. Finally, his eyes met mine. I knew he didn't realize who I was so I lifted my hand and waved at him. Jason's eyebrows drew together in confusion as he crossed the room towards me.

He stopped right in front of me. "I'm sorry, do I know you?"

I smiled at him. "It's starting to feel more and more as if you might be the only one who truly does."

A couple seconds later he broke into a huge smile, picked me up and spun me around. "I knew you'd come, Quinn," he whispered in my ear.

"Honestly, I didn't think I'd make it."

"I sent a car for you."

"Yeah, my stepmother and stepsisters took that. I found my way, though."

Jason set me down, took my hands in his and gave me a thorough once over. "You're so beautiful. I mean I love the way you normally look, it suits you but this...this is something."

I blushed and broke eye contact with him. The last thing I wanted to do tonight was act shy or awkward. Jason would be leaving Savannah soon. I needed to throw caution to the wind and finally take a chance on something. Tonight, anything felt possible.

Looking him boldly in the eyes, I said, "It's so beautiful. I never went to prom, but I imagine it was like this. Well, except for the belles and soldiers."

Jason drew his brows together in concern. "You never went to prom?"

"I didn't have the easiest life in high school. Who would have asked me?"

He touched my cheek. "Me. C'mon let me show you off."

I let him pull me along even as I protested. "Jason, I'm not sure that's such a good idea. I don't want anyone to know who I am."

He winked at me. "Who says they have to? No one can tell with that mask on. What should your name be?"

Letting myself sink into the fantasy, I pulled out the first name that came to mind. "Margaret." It was because of her I was here. I figured it was fair.

"Margaret it is." He escorted me up to a tall man with a full head of salt-and-pepper hair standing with a couple of minor actors I recognized from movies and television.

I prayed I'd be able to pull this off.

"Stan, I'd like you to meet a true Southern belle. This is Margaret." Jason motioned to me and I smiled. "Margaret, this is Stan Cooper the director."

Stan returned the smile. He was a handsome man with twinkling blue eyes. I felt at ease with him.

"Leave it to Jason to find a genuine belle in this beautiful city." He reached for my hand and grasped it in his. "You are a vision."

Lost in the role I answered in my deepest accent. "Thank you, Mr. Cooper. I hope ya'll are enjoyin' Savannah."

Jason watched with a huge grin on his face as he introduced me to the group. One of the actresses even complimented my accent, declaring it was the hardest accent she ever had to learn. I loved the attention, I'll fully admit it.

Even watching Jason interact with these people he saw everyday was illuminating. His confidence was sexy and he had a great sarcastic sense of humor I'd already seen hints of. This was Jason in his element and it fit him well.

Stan's wife Danielle laid her hand on my arm and spoke quietly, "That is the most gorgeous dress I've seen all night. Where on earth did you get it?"

"Oh, it's been in the family for generations. Every time I pull it out of storage, I'm amazed it has survived this long."

It was mostly the truth. Still unable to comprehend how Margaret came up with a dress like this, I was half-afraid I wore a moth-eaten rag and everyone was looking at an illusion. Nervous laughter almost bubbled up out of me.

Before Danielle could speak again, Jason pulled me aside. "Sorry guys, she's all mine now."

He led me towards the dance floor through a crowd of curious and envious stares. I tried to remain alert for Marietta or the twins but I was walking in a dream. I wanted to remember every detail, the way his hand felt covering mine, or how the light from the chandelier reflected off his dark hair.

"You were awesome. Who knew you were such an actress?" Jason joked.

Before I had a chance to answer, I heard voices calling his name.

"Jason!"

"Over here!"

"Can we get one picture?"

I followed the sounds and saw a herd of photographers held back by a barricade. Even before Jason turned, the flashbulbs started flashing. I stood frozen in place, unsure of what to do.

Jason pressed close and whispered in my ear. "We'll give them one. Just smile and pretend I'm the most charming man you've ever met."

He wrapped his arm around my waist and held me tight. His remark did bring a smile to my face and I faced the cameras. The flashes were distracting and blinding. I gained new respect for how he lived his life. I was a fish in an aquarium, on display for the entire world.

After a minute or so, Jason raised his hand in a wave. "That's enough guys. Let me enjoy this fine party with a beautiful girl."

Finally, we made it to the dance floor as more shouts followed us.

"What's your name, sweetie?"

"Who's your date, Jason?"

He pulled me into his arms as the music changed into a slow, haunting song. I was aware of everyone watching us, whispering and wondering who the girl was in Jason's arms. I didn't care.

The reporters shook my resolve a little but I closed my eyes and let the music settle over me. For that blissful moment of time, we existed in our own bubble.

I lost track of how long we danced or to how many songs but when Jason took my hand and led me out to the terrace, it felt like I'd been in his arms for days.

As we passed the floor-to-ceiling windows, I caught sight of our reflection. I remembered the first time I saw Jason and me together in the reflection of a store window. That girl didn't belong. This girl did.

This girl's eyes sparkled with excitement and she glowed from the inside. I watched as the Jason in the reflection gazed down at her with an expression that stole my breath away. He appeared to be a man in love. A man who saw nothing but the girl at his side.

He pulled me out into the warm night air before I could dwell on that. The strains of "Georgia on My Mind" drifted out behind us. Even the night was perfect. The sky twinkled with stars, the cicadas gave off a symphony of background music and the heat had faded to the perfect mix of warmth and humidity that held you in a heated embrace. I loved the feeling. It was as if the night had arms and all it wanted to do was hold me in them forever. Whatever people said about the brutal heat of the South, a night like this, complete with its warm embrace, always felt so romantic to me.

And I was sharing it with a person who'd taken me by complete surprise.

As Jason stood close to me, more than anything I wanted to rip off my mask. It still felt like I was hiding a little with it on. I wanted him to see me without any masks on, real or imagined.

"I'm so glad you're here. I've been standing around all night, talking to these people and the only one I wanted to share it with was you."

I gasped. "I don't know what to say to you when you talk that way."

He brushed his thumb over my lips and I trembled. "You don't have to say anything, Quinn. All I know is, when you waved at me and I realized it was you, something clicked inside me. I was the luckiest man in the room."

"Jason, I—."

He interrupted me by putting a finger up to stop me. "Quinn you don't have to come up with an answer for everything. Sometimes you just have to give in and trust and feel."

Then he leaned in and kissed me.

I wanted to remember it all; the smell, the taste, the feel, but every single thought emptied my head. The magical things I experienced and witnessed tonight didn't come close to the sensations that kiss sent coursing through my veins. The kiss was slow and devastating. I felt my blood come alive. It was a slow burn, starting at my lips and spreading into the very core of me.

The feelings were so contradictory. My head felt light as a feather but my body trembled. I was drowning but I never wanted it to end. When Jason broke away, we both struggled to catch our breath. His face was inches from mine and all I wanted to do was pull him close again. I knew I'd compare every kiss from that day forward to his.

Unfortunately, I couldn't dwell too long on the kiss. I saw Suzie and Anna over his shoulder heading in our direction and it was like someone tossing a bucket of cold water over my head.

"Crap, I've got to get out of here before they see me," I mumbled. "Don't look but my stepsisters are headed our way. I apologize in advance for their behavior."

He kissed me quick one last time. "Let me know when you're home and safe."

I hustled off the terrace, to the side of the building, and caught a cab out front. Hysterical laughter bubbled up as I almost lost my shoe getting in the car. How ironic would that be?

During the entire ride home I didn't stop smiling. I hadn't spent much time at the ball, but every second with Jason felt like a lifetime. It was a precious gift I'd remember until the day I died. And probably even after that.

The house was empty when I returned. I rushed up to the attic and shut the door behind me. The lock engaged by itself and I heard the same heavy piece of furniture move in front of it.

Alone in my room, I delayed undressing by texting Jason. The sooner I took the dress off the sooner the night would end.

Finally, I changed and put on my pajamas. Then, the adrenaline crashed and my body was heavy with exhaustion. I curled up in bed and basked in the lingering warmth of Jason's kiss.

I should be with him, out until the sun comes up, I thought sadly. But here I was, curled up in bed alone and hiding like a coward.

Chapter Twenty-Two

The next couple of days after the ball were frighteningly quiet. Marietta wasn't around much and I wondered where she disappeared to for hours at a time. When I did see her, the darkness appeared to be much less significant, almost muted. I knew it didn't mean things were over.

Actually, I got the feeling Catherine was laying in wait, letting me think I was safe. She enjoyed toying with me.

I knew better than to relax. The necklace Margaret gave me never left my neck. Whenever I was close to Marietta I tucked it away. I didn't even want to think of what would happen if Catherine saw me wearing it. I knew I was playing with fire but I didn't feel so alone when I wore it.

One afternoon, Jason and I were sitting in one of the parks near our house. The many squares of green space dotting the historic part of town gave us plenty of private places to hang out. When the city was founded in 1733 by James Oglethorpe, there were originally four squares whose main function was to provide space for military maneuvers. Over time, as Savannah grew, more and more were added and today there were twenty-two squares. They were one more thing that made Savannah so unique.

We sat there for a couple hours and I ran lines with Jason for the intense ending they were filming later that night. It was fun and comfortable, and safe being with him. Isaac, the bodyguard assigned to Jason, kept to himself. I was glad we hadn't needed him yet but I knew it was only a matter of time before that part of Jason's life collided with our budding relationship.

He didn't give me a chance to feel awkward about our kiss, which I was thankful for. It surprised me how much I'd changed in the couple of months since I met him.

"I think I'm finally getting used to this heat. It forces you to slow down. I've decided this slow, lazy lifestyle appeals to me." Jason brushed my hair out of my face. "How are things at the house?"

I shrugged. "It's been okay. Marietta's been suspiciously absent which makes me more nervous. I need to figure out how to fight this thing."

"What do you mean, fight it? You can't be serious." Again, I suspected he didn't understand my feelings or my need to see it through to the end.

"I'm very serious. What else should I do, ignore it and run away? I'm the one left to finish this."

Jason stood up and started to pace in front of me. "Well, can't we bring in a priest or exorcist or something? There has to be someone you can get to help. This thing already tried to kill you once and I won't lose someone else I care about."

I walked over to him and put my hand on his cheek. "Who? Talk to me, Jason."

He looked at me with such a huge well of sadness behind his eyes. He took a deep breath and tried to compose himself.

"My brother," he began softly. "We were on our way to go snowboarding. I grew up in Colorado and learned to drive on icy, snowy roads. I remember him talking about how much he hated being a freshman in high school. I was a sophomore and had already gone through it so I was giving him advice. Then, some stupid country song came on the radio. We were laughing and singing along to it.

"No matter how many times I go over it, I can't pinpoint what went wrong. I wasn't driving fast or recklessly but an oncoming car drifted into our lane. Trying to avoid it, I lost control of the Suburban and hit a patch of ice. We rolled and the car came to rest with the passenger side crushed into a tree. I tried to get Dylan out, to wake him up but he never came to. I never got to tell him I was sorry."

I held him as he cried. Instinctively I knew this wasn't something he shared with most people. I understood loss but nothing like what he'd experienced.

"It's okay," I whispered. "I'm sure he knew and I'm sure he doesn't blame you."

He pulled back and wiped his eyes before laying his forehead to mine. "I tell myself that constantly. We were close and deep down I know he understands but it doesn't stop me from questioning everything that happened that day. I only had my license a couple of months but my parents trusted me, letting me take the car that day. We lived half an hour from the ski hill. I'd already made the trip twice that month."

"What happened to the other driver?" I asked. Most of the details of the article I read were pretty hazy.

"The driver never stopped and they never found him. I remember wanting to feel some kind of justice, even though I believed most of the blame was on me."

"Blame and guilt are funny things. Even with Mama dying of a brain aneurism and Daddy of a heart attack, I wondered if it was my fault. Could I have been a better daughter? Did they love me too much? We imagine there's something we could have done different even in an impossible situation."

"I know." Jason sighed heavily. "The last couple years I've come to terms with the fact it wasn't my fault but there's still guilt. I will always have guilt. And I will always second guess everything about that day."

"I think it's only natural, Jason. So did you leave Colorado to get away from everything?"

"I had to get away from there. The memories were too much so I managed to graduate early and started over in LA the minute I turned eighteen. I got a job pretty quick and I guess the rest is history."

"Is this why you're so interested in the paranormal? Because you want to find out what happens after?"

"Yeah, when I first learned we were going to be filming here I thought I'd finally have a chance to find out more about what happens when you die. Is Dylan still back home or did he move on? All I want is some answers."

"It's kind of why I started investigating. Whatever my capabilities are as far as sensing things, I still want to know more about my parents. One of the things I've learned is the answers aren't always out there. I've done everything I possibly can to contact my parents and I've never felt anything, not even a twinge."

"The logical part of me realizes it's something I'll never find out. It doesn't make me stop though. You've shown me more than I ever imagined and it helps learning about spirits and their world. That's why I don't want anything to happen to you. What you're dealing with is dangerous."

I sat back down on the bench. I knew he wanted me to be safe but the reality of the situation still loomed before me.

"Jason, you have to understand, I cannot get on with my life the way I want until this is finished. There's a reason Catherine's here now and I can't let her win."

Once again, he sat beside me and hung his head. After a couple seconds passed, he looked at me and said, "I realize how important this is to you, that isn't lost on me but I'm not going to let you do it on your own. Whether I help you or someone else, you won't be alone. Maybe I can call one of these paranormal groups, set up a meeting. I'm more than happy to use my money or so-called fame to help."

"You can try but I don't think even you could get a meeting right away."

"Wanna make a bet? Just watch and learn." He pulled out his iPhone and began typing in some information. When I leaned over to peek, he hid it from me. After a few more minutes, he placed a call.

"Hi. Magnolia Paranormal Society? My name is Jason Preston and I'm in town this summer filming a movie. Yeah, that's me. I was wondering if I could set up an appointment to talk to one of your investigators. I think it would help me be better prepared for this role."

As he listened, he winked at me and I rolled my eyes.

"Actually, would you be available today? I was hoping to get this done as soon as possible. I have a big scene coming up and want to get it right. Perfect, yeah I can find it. I'll see you there." He ended the call and said, "And that is how it's done."

"I can't believe it was that easy. It must have been a woman."

"What exactly does that mean?" He pretended to look innocent.

"You know what I mean. You have to be aware of your effect on the female gender. My bet is you talked to a girl who just answers the phone. She found out it was you and is going to pretend to be an investigator. Simple."

"You're pretty sure of yourself aren't ya? We'll just wait and see." Jason stood and pulled me up with him. We approached his bodyguard, Isaac, hand in hand. "The investigator is meeting us in an hour."

Chapter Twenty-Three

Avoiding the more crowded parts of the downtown area, we slowly made our way to the small café where the investigator was meeting us.

Jason and I arrived first and took one of the back tables.

"I'm kind of nervous about this."

Jason leaned over and took my hands in his. "Why? I thought you decided this would be the smartest thing to do."

"I'm not exactly an open book kind of girl. Sharing this with you and Abby was different. This is some random person."

"I get that and I'm proud of you. Just keep your eye on the end prize, having your house to yourself once and for all."

We were silent for a little while before he asked about our investigations. "What's the best piece of evidence you've found? I think those ghost hunting shows on TV have really brought stuff like this into the public eye, before it wasn't as 'cool' to be interested in ghosts."

"You're right, it's become more acceptable. I think the best thing we've found was the dark shape of a person standing in a doorway at Moon River. It's a video and you can clearly see it peer around the edge of the doorway. The stuff I've picked up at the house isn't as good. That might be because I'm too used to what goes on there, but I'll never get used to the disembodied voices. A voice coming out of thin air is disturbing."

"I don't even want to imagine the things you've seen and heard over the years."

No, he didn't. I wished my ability to hear spirits was getting weaker instead of stronger. Maybe the person we were waiting on could help with that as well.

A younger man in his mid-twenties stopped at the table. He had spiky blond hair and wore black framed glasses. For some reason, I relaxed even though I was expecting someone much older. I sat back and unclenched my fists as Jason elbowed me and whispered, "See, it's not a woman."

"Jason?" he greeted. "I'm Travis."

Jason stood up and shook the man's hand. "Thanks for getting here so quickly, I really appreciate it. Have a seat."

Travis sat as Jason introduced me and I tried not to fidget too much.

"Alright, I have to admit I'm very curious about what you want to talk to me about. You said it was for a movie?"

Clearing his throat nervously, Jason admitted, "Well, I wasn't completely honest with you on the phone. I do have questions but it's not for a movie, or even for me. It's about Quinn here. She needs some help."

"Why didn't you just tell me that to begin with?" Travis gave me an uncertain smile.

"That's my fault. I thought if you knew who I was it would get us a meeting faster. It's a serious situation and I have to say I'm a little worried about her being hurt."

"Hurt? I'm not sure I'm following you."

"Why don't I let Quinn explain?"

I took a deep breath and launched into the things that were happening to me. I couldn't read the expression on Travis's face but he was listening intently.

When I finished, I watched Travis mulling over my story. I could tell some of the stuff took him by surprise, as well as Jason. I didn't leave anything out and felt Jason tense up beside me as I talked about the incident with the grave.

Finally, Travis spoke. "I'm glad you called me. This *is* a very dangerous situation."

"Yes, I'm learning today just how dangerous." Jason directed towards me. To Travis, he said, "So is there anything you can tell us about why this is happening and how we can stop it?"

"Actually, it might have been happening longer than you realize, Quinn."

"What do you mean?" I asked him.

"With this kind of haunting, more often than not it's a multigenerational event. Have any other family members been plagued by a spirit of some kind?"

"No, I don't think so. Both sets of my grandparents died when I was young and same with my parents. I have an aunt and uncle but they live on the other side of the country. Neither of my parents ever mentioned anything about spirits that I can remember. Mama always told me stories about the paranormal side of the city but I'm not sure if she meant anything specific with her."

Travis thought for a second. "Your dad was a Roberts, right?" I nodded. "And he was an only child?"

"Yes. Mama wasn't, though."

"Do you think this spirit only harasses the females in the family?" Jason's question surprised me and lit my curiosity.

"I'm not entirely sure but it's possible. You said she mentioned wanting destroy you or the family. Maybe she's been there all along but now she's concentrating on you because you're so vulnerable."

I tried not to make a face at Travis' usage of the word 'vulnerable'. As much as I hated the word and in no way saw myself as that, I understood what he meant. I was the last Roberts and Catherine had the opportunity to exact the ultimate revenge. Not that it made me feel any better.

"I might be able to ask Margaret if she knows about anyone else being affected by Catherine."

They both shot me looks of disbelief before Jason said, "I should be used to this by now, I guess. Do you think you can contact her?"

"Not sure, but it's worth a shot." I turned towards Travis. "Is there a way Catherine can be stopped?"

"Yes, I believe so. It's basically treated like a demonic possession. We have to force the spirit out of your stepmother. Somewhere along the line, your stepmother accepted or invited the spirit in, that's the only way a possession this powerful could happen."

"I don't understand. Why would Marietta invite this in? I've seen how it feeds off her. It's draining the life out of her."

A picture of Marietta flashed into my head. Her pale lips, sunken eyes and vacant expression caused her to resemble the walking dead. There was no way she wanted that.

"She probably wasn't aware of what she was agreeing to. The spirit of Catherine might have the ability to alter a person's sense of reality. You witnessed that yourself in the cemetery. Catherine could very well be keeping your stepmother in a state of illusion. When she looks in the mirror, she won't see how it's affecting her physically."

"That's disturbing." I figured he had to be right about the illusion. Any woman as high maintenance as Marietta would likely have a meltdown at seeing her reflection and her dark roots showing.

"So basically in order to get Catherine's spirit to leave Marietta, we also have to convince Marietta to allow that. Does that make sense? This isn't only about Catherine."

I must have looked worried because Travis continued, "This is going to be hard. I'm not going to lie to you. It might not even work the first time. What I need you to do now is find out as much as you can about Catherine and if she's done this before. I'll do some research on my end and we'll meet back here in three days, on Thursday. Does that sound good?"

Jason and I both nodded. I could tell Travis was anxious to get started and after he left I couldn't help but breathe a sigh of relief.

Jason grinned at me. "See, I told you it would be a good idea."

Chapter Twenty-Four

My birthday was a week away and my battered nerves were starting to get to me.

Every time I closed my eyes to sleep, I expected Catherine to come at me with a vengeance. I kept looking over my shoulder, waiting for her to attack from behind. Each day that went by without incident or, at least a major incident, frayed my patience more.

I felt like a sitting duck cornered in a dark alley with nowhere to go.

I was on my knees in the dining room, trying to remove a scuffmark from the old hardwood floor when a chill settled over me. Goosebumps covered my arms before I noticed I was no longer alone. I smelled the foul river stench before I saw her. Marietta hovered over me but I saw no trace of her. This, I knew, was Catherine and I braced myself for what was about to happen.

"Where did you get that?" Again, it was the strange, creepy voice speaking to me, only this time with tightly controlled anger.

I glanced to where she pointed and my heart stopped. As I'd bent over to scrub the floor, the necklace Margaret gave me swung free from my shirt. It was right there in plain sight, twinkling in the afternoon light.

Rising to my feet, I tensed my body to run. "I found it upstairs, in the attic," I answered weakly.

A strange, almost wistful look transformed her face. "I wore that on my wedding day, only I wasn't marrying the man I always pictured when I'd think of forever."

"Jackson." This was the only time Catherine hadn't threatened me and I vaguely wondered if I had an opportunity to reason with her.

Tears sprang up in Marietta's vacant eyes and she clutched her chest. "Jackson. Yes, he was the man I should have married. I waited for him but my parents had other plans for me."

I swallowed. "No one could have known he was still alive."

"I knew. I knew in my heart he was out there, somewhere. The day of my wedding, I'd planned on running away. William was a monster but no one seemed to care. All they cared about was settling a debt with me as the price."

Her shadow swooped up and darkened, throwing the room into a kaleidoscope of light and dark.

"It probably hurt your parents more than you know to marry you off to him."

Then it all changed.

The room darkened, turning it to night. The shadows cast crazy patterns on Marietta's face. It made me think of a scary clown in a horror movie. Then, the temperature in the room dropped. I saw my breath and my teeth started chattering.

I remembered as a kid watching a movie alone one night called Poltergeist. It scared the crap out of me. What made me think of it now was the way the atmosphere in the house changed so quickly, exactly like in the movie. I half expected to see the chairs in the room stack themselves or the tree outside the window to come to life and try to devour me.

Only now, it was Marietta who wanted to rip me apart.

"They had a choice! They could have given him this house instead of their firstborn daughter. I was handed over to him like nothing more than a piece of property," she screamed.

Marietta's hand reached out to grab the necklace. The minute her fingers grazed the gold pendant, it sparked.

She wrenched her hand back and roared, "Give me that!"

I shook my head in a quick movement and tried to inch my way out of the room.

What little light was left in the room got sucked out and the house literally shuddered. An icy cold breeze sprung up around me and picked up force, placing me in the middle of a tornado.

The river stench grew, thick and suffocating. My vision blurred as the wind intensified. I had no idea where she was. The darkness lightened some and I saw objects flying through the room, caught in the maelstrom that Catherine was fueling.

In the corner Marietta's body stood staring at the wall, an empty vessel swaying with the gusts of air battering her. Catherine's shadow became a separate entity and rushed at me. Pain ripped through every inch of me and my skin burned. Invisible flames licked at my skin, spreading an intense pain over every inch of me. I came close to passing out.

From what felt like a hundred miles away, I sensed George enter the room and move towards Catherine. I wanted to tell him to go, that she was too strong for him, but the agony of the searing flames locked my mouth shut and rendered me speechless.

The shadow beat him back and his spirit disappeared. There was a loud crash and the sound of broken glass as the wind and the burning sensation intensified.

Pain erased most of the thoughts from my head but I was aware of the fear. Whenever Catherine attacked me, I feared in my heart that it would be the last time. Twice now, I'd said my goodbyes and made peace with the death drawing close. Something always stopped it. I was afraid this really was the last time. I was also afraid it wasn't and I'd have to wait for the next attack. I was afraid the relentless scorching of the invisible flames would chase away my sanity.

Through the fog of my waning consciousness I saw the shape of Catherine, vaguely human in form, coming at me.

This is finally it, I thought.

I said goodbye to Jason in my head as the shadow moved to envelope me.

It didn't have a chance.

A bright light burst into the room, same as before. The pain let up slightly and I knew Margaret was there. Catherine was forced back into a corner but she didn't stay there.

She must have gained power since the first time because she merely gathered herself back up and came at me again. I worried Margaret didn't have the energy to hold her back twice and the tiny spark of hope I had of getting out alive, faded.

This time, the shadow came up short. My thoughts clouded over as excruciating pain sliced through my body. On my left, I detected someone else in the room.

Jackson.

Little by little, the burning faded and the wind died down to a heavy breeze. I dropped to my knees and curled up, wrapping my arms around myself protectively.

Jackson walked into the room and stopped in front of me, blocking Catherine's advance. I watched as her shadow pulled itself together into the shape of a woman. Briefly, I wished I knew what she looked like. I got a sense of long flowing brown hair, but it disappeared as quick as it came.

"Catherine, you cannot do this." The soft voice of a young man echoed on the breeze.

A quiet sob burst out. "Jackson, darling."

He cut her off. "You must stop. This isn't you. The woman I loved more than life itself would not kill an innocent girl."

I was familiar enough with Catherine's moods to realize that ticked her off.

"How dare you stand there and judge me," she snapped. "You can't begin to imagine what I had to endure. No one cared at all about what he did to me."

Jackson took a hesitant step towards her. "I would give anything to change our past, you know that."

"I died trying to run away to meet you. He caught me and beat me and dumped me in the river like trash. You told me you'd protect me. You told me you'd take me away from him!"

I wondered if this was the first time they were speaking of the tragic events surrounding her death. Their spirits appeared to exist under the same roof for so long. Were they aware of each other? Was this the first time Jackson was able to communicate with her? It made me sad for some reason.

"Sweetheart, I would have killed him to save you. I would've gladly given my life for yours, but that has nothing to do with Quinn. She is an innocent."

The breeze picked up again and I felt her try to force him out of the room. Jackson did not move which only made her more irate. Once again, the house vibrated with her power and I believed it would come crashing down. Jackson stood his ground, though.

Catherine screamed in frustration and abruptly, everything stopped. The silence was deafening. By the time I realized it was over, all I saw was Marietta walking out of the room, staring vacantly ahead.

But I heard Catherine's voice in my head. *This is far from over. You will pay for this!*

Great, now she probably thinks her guy picked me over her. Not a good sign.

I glanced in the direction of Jackson, finally getting a good look at him. He was gorgeous.

His dark blond hair curled around the edges of his Confederate hat and even though he was a mere spirit, his blue eyes stood out from a chiseled face. He also had a few days worth of stubble and holes in his uniform. I could see why Catherine fell so hard for him.

I had to have been in shock to even notice something that foolish after what happened.

Jackson's spirit faded dimmer and dimmer as I sensed him kneel down beside me. An intense wave of calmness rolled over me. My thoughts cleared, giving me the chance to double check whether or not I'd actually been on fire.

When I felt strong enough to stand, I got a good look at the dining room. Or what was left of it. The glass doors of the hutch were busted and so was every piece of heirloom china inside of it. Glass shards scattered the floor and the hundred year old dining room table lay shattered in hundreds of pieces.

I gaped at it in wonder, trying to figure out how I would ever explain this to anyone.

Then, I remembered Jackson. I turned in his direction. He seemed heartbroken.

"I can't ever begin to thank you."

He nodded sullenly and walked out of the destroyed room.

Exhaustion picked that moment to come crashing down on me and I swayed on my feet. Every single ounce of energy was gone from my body. Instead of trudging up to my bed, I went to the broom closet to try to start cleaning up the mess.

Chapter Twenty-Five

I was sitting at the breakfast bar with a bowl of cereal when Anna came in and plucked an apple from the fruit bowl. Instead of turning and leaving as I wanted her to, she leaned against the counter across from me.

With my spoon halfway to my mouth, I sat frozen, waiting for whatever would come next.

She looked at the door to the kitchen, as if making sure we were alone and asked, "Have you noticed anything weird about my mom lately?"

I looked in her troubled blue eyes and sighed. This was not a conversation I wanted to be having with her, mostly because she'd never believe me. The other reason was because I didn't need anyone else involved or in danger.

"Not really. What do you mean, Anna?" I saw she didn't believe me and I didn't blame her. My lie sounded very unconvincing.

She moved closer to me. "I know you read a lot of books on ghosts. I've seen you with them. I think something is messing with her, something in this house."

Her voice reflected how uncomfortable she was talking to me. It took me by complete surprise. I had no clue how I was going to dodge or even explain this one. Before I could reply, she spoke again.

"You don't have anything to do with it, do you? I mean, Suzie has convinced herself you can do stuff like that, but not me. I'm giving you the benefit of the doubt here."

I stared into my cereal bowl and thought over what to say. Anna was coming to me for help. Maybe she could be open minded enough to hear some of it. No way would I ever tell her all of it.

"What have you noticed?" I asked her.

"She's not there anymore. She forgets things and sometimes won't even recognize us. Then, sometimes," she looked very nervous. "Sometimes I see this shadow behind her. I don't know how to explain it. She even disappears for hours and we can't find her. Then, there was whatever happened in the dining room yesterday. You cleaned it up, but she didn't even bat an eye. The table and dishes were old, the kind of thing she keeps track of. That's not how she would have normally reacted."

It was sobering to hear Anna talk about what was going on with Marietta. The fact that she could see the shadow surprised me, too. She must be more open-minded than I ever gave her credit for. As far as what happened yesterday in the dining room, Anna was right. Marietta should have blown a gasket at that. In fact, all morning I'd been waiting for it.

I pushed my cereal bowl away, trying to come up with the best way to talk to her. "I can at least tell you it's not the house."

"How?"

"Look, I'd love to talk to you about this, but I'm afraid you're only going to use it against me as usual."

Anna took a step forward as she said, "We've done some awful things to you and maybe one day we can talk about that, but this isn't about you or me. It's about my mom."

I wanted to believe her so badly. If Travis's plan didn't work, Anna and Suzie had a right to hear about how it would affect them. Whether or not they saw the truth in it was up to them.

"I think I know what's going on but I need you to be open minded. You've lived in this house long enough to know that there are spirits still living here. I'm sure you've heard them before."

"You mean the doors slamming and the footsteps and the shadows?"

"Yes. What they do might be annoying but it's never anything mean or harmful to you guys." I paused and had second thoughts about how much to say. "But there are spirits or ghosts who are malicious and want to do harm. I strongly believe one of those spirits has some kind of um, influence on Marietta."

"What exactly do you mean by 'influence'?" Her face paled and her eyes widened in fear.

I took my cereal bowl over to the sink and leaned against the counter next to her. "I mean some kind of possession."

I thought she was going to pass out as the implication of what I said sank in. She struggled to speak and I saw her fighting tears.

"Like the Exorcist?" She finally squeaked out.

"No, no, nothing like that. That was a demonic possession. A demonic entity can possess a person but so can a spirit, a ghost. The shadow you mentioned, I think it's what controls her at times. Can you tell me anything more specific about what you've noticed?"

She sniffed and wiped her eyes. "I've noticed it for a while now but always thought it was something temporary. It's gotten much worse lately. The salon called the other day to see if she would be in. Apparently, mom hadn't been in for three days. She forgets about the pageant and though it sounds selfish, I don't mean it that way. Mom had this timetable and schedule of when our costumes and stuff needed to be done. You know how she was, one of those over-involved pageant moms. Now she doesn't even care, even though I'm only doing it for her and Suzie."

Her words intrigued me. She always seemed as excited about the pageant as Suzie. I never would have imagined it was all a front. I wondered what else about Anna I'd incorrectly assumed.

"The shadow around her gives me the creeps. She gets this vacant look in her eyes, like she doesn't see me standing in front of her. There are times I don't even recognize her. That shadow thing is cold and," she searched for the word, "vengeful. It wants to hurt someone."

"Do you believe that, Anna?"

"How can I not? You said it yourself, it's hard to live here and not notice there's more going on. If you repeat that to anyone, you'll be sorry. Now please, tell me what is going on."

"The spirit controlling your mama is named Catherine Roberts. She is one of my ancestors, forced to marry a bad man who killed her and dumped her in the river. Catherine blames her family and in turn, blames me. She wants the life she was denied and to end the Roberts family with me."

"By ending your family with you, do you mean to kill you?" I nodded. "So basically, all this is your fault."

"No, it's not my fault. I didn't ask for this," I said heatedly. "Catherine has tried to kill me three times already. I'm terrified that the next time will be the last. If anything, it's Marietta's fault for inviting this thing in."

"What do you mean? She would never do that."

"With this kind of possession she did. Catherine must have offered Marietta something tempting in return for her help. In all fairness, I don't think your mama had any idea what she would be getting herself into. Catherine is strong because she feeds off Marietta. I'm worried about how much more she can take. Catherine grows stronger every day."

Tears streamed down Anna's face. I wanted to offer her some comfort but the thought of it exhausted me.

"How do we help her?" she asked.

"I'm working on that. I've talked to a paranormal investigator who says he can help rid Marietta of Catherine's spirit. We have to lure her to where the grave is. Regardless of what you think of me, I want to help Marietta."

"Quinn, I've been really hateful toward you all these years. It's a little late to ask for any kind of forgiveness but know that I did feel bad about it, most of the time. I get caught up in being this person, especially in school and it's impossible to get out. I'm not strong like you are."

"I'm not as strong as you think," I said as I laughed ironically. "I'm scared to death about all of this. Believe me when I say I wish I could run away from here and never look back. But I can't do that to Marietta."

She was quiet for a while. "How did it try to kill you, Quinn?"

"Which time?" I tried to joke with her about it, but all I saw were her eyes widened in fear. Probably not the best approach to take with her. "The first time Catherine strangled me somehow. I felt the fingers on my neck but it was only shadow. Next, she tried to bury me alive or at least give me the illusion I was being buried alive. Yesterday, she came at me in the dining room but one of the other ghosts intervened."

It was a lot for her to process and I instantly regretted saying anything.

"So that's what happened to the table?"

I nodded, surprised. Apparently she believed me.

"Let me help." Anna said with a new determination in her eyes.

"Help with what?"

"With Mom, I want to be there. Maybe it will give her more to fight for. It makes sense, right?"

She surprised me again. I was lost in this alternate universe where Anna and I were equals, maybe even friends. I considered her idea and saw the sense in it. Marietta loved her girls. It might be the right thing to compel her to fight.

"It is a good idea but I'll need to run it by the guy who's going to be doing it. He might not want any outsiders there."

"I'm not an outsider. She's my mom."

"You're right and I'll tell him I agree. I'll let you know tomorrow or the next day."

Anna turned to leave but stopped. She looked over her shoulder and flashed me a sad smile. "Thanks Quinn. I'm glad I could talk to you about this."

Now I just needed to convince Travis when we met with him in a couple days.

Chapter Twenty-Six

Jason asked me to meet him a couple blocks from where the movie was filming. He wanted to explore the surrounding neighborhood and take in the unique Savannah architecture.

The afternoon was sweltering. I passed a few sweating tourists strolling the area with their cameras and street maps. They looked miserable in the heat and humidity and I gave an encouraging smile to a mother who looked like she might drop at any second.

Lost in memories of vacations, I reached the square where we were meeting. Jason was already there but he was laughing with a gorgeous blond.

Frozen in place, I watched them. My instincts told me to walk away, to leave and pretend I didn't see them together, but that felt a bit excessive. I didn't have any special hold or claim on Jason. Jealousy wasn't what kept me rooted to my spot; it was curiosity.

He was an entirely different person, so carefree and relaxed. We didn't get much opportunity to laugh since we put a lot of focus was on my problems. I felt guilty and wanted to show him he could have fun with me, that I could be lighthearted when I wasn't being haunted by a hundred-and-fifty-year-old ghost.

The girl made me curious, too. She didn't put up a wall the way I did. Granted, I had grown better since the ball but I was still wary of trusting him. Or maybe I was wary of trusting *myself* with him. I hadn't quite figured that one out yet. Her laughter drifted back to me and it sounded familiar. Then, when she turned her face, disbelief washed over me.

It was Anna.

A heavy ball grew in the center of my stomach. It wasn't that Jason was talking to another girl, which I'm certain he did every day. And it wasn't because Anna was at least attempting to be civil to me lately. I think it had to do with the fact that even after all the time we'd spent together, I didn't know much about Jason. And I wanted to. We kissed and talked as much as we could but there was more to him than that.

I decided to make a conscious effort to learn more about him. If I wanted to start living my life, here was my opportunity. Life was about taking chances. Besides, I really didn't like the idea of him with another girl regardless of who she was. It made me want to fight for him.

They stood up and Anna ran her hand down his arm before walking away. He watched after her and shook his head. Then Jason searched the grassy area and saw me.

I waved as I made my way toward him, a little embarrassed that he'd caught me watching him.

"That girl you were talking to is one of my stepsisters."

He narrowed his eyes and dropped his chin to his chest. "Crap, Quinn, I'm sorry. I had no idea."

"Where did you run into her?"

"She cornered me about a block away and kept talking about that stupid pageant. I couldn't get rid of her."

I shrugged my shoulder halfheartedly. "Anna hasn't been that bad lately. Suzie's still a first class witch but Anna has reached out to me a couple times. She's worried about her mama and doesn't really have anyone to talk to about it. She's involved now anyway. I need to get used to it. Be thankful it wasn't Suzie you ran into."

"You're scaring me," he joked.

Not wanting to talk about Anna anymore, I changed the subject. "So what did you want to do today? See more of the neighborhoods, right?"

"I did, but I think we should drive out to the ocean instead." He held up a set of car keys. "I have wheels for the day. Do you have time?"

I smiled. I had always loved the beach but didn't get to visit much. As close as Savannah was to the ocean, it was a shame not to take advantage of it.

"For the chance to go to the beach with you, I'll risk it. We can go out to Tybee Island. There are beautiful beaches, forts and even a lighthouse. If no one is home, I'd love to stop at my house and grab my camera."

Jason beamed. "No problem. Let's go."

I was lucky. The house was empty, at least of the living. I stopped long enough to leave a note for Marietta saying I'd be gone all day to Tybee Island with Abby and her mom. She might not like it, neither would Catherine for that matter, but I was grasping life by the horns. Spending a day at the beach with Jason would be worth the consequences when I got home.

Jason's car was a Ford Mustang convertible; a car I thought he looked perfect in. As we joined US-80 East, I leaned my head back and enjoyed the sun on my face and the wind in my hair. I turned towards Jason and lifted my camera to snap a quick, unguarded photo of him driving.

"Hey careful now, that picture could be worth a lot of money one day." He said as he shot me a quick grin.

"Please, you have your trusty disguise on today. I doubt anyone would believe it's you. Besides, maybe this movie will be the peak of your career."

The sound of his laughter warmed my insides. This was turning out to be such a different day than I imagined. I felt light and free. Worries about Catherine and the other things going on in my life were already trying to invade my happy space, but I didn't let them. Today was about me.

"There will be a turn coming up on your left for Fort Pulaski. It's a really cool fort that was used to defend the city during the War."

"That sounds awesome. I love you say the 'War', like it was the only war fought."

"It was to those who live in the South."

I pointed out the turn-off and Jason crossed over a bridge into the Fort Pulaski Historical Monument. The old stone fort was surrounded by a water-filled moat and the sides still showed the deep gouges and pockmarks from Yankee fire.

"Dylan would've loved this place. He was in that stage where he read about war and built models of battleships. In fact, he wanted to go on a family vacation to see each battlefield in the U.S." Jason shook his head. I loved hearing him talk about his brother. The more he opened up, the more pieces I acquired of Dylan's memory.

We spent about an hour wandering the grounds. Old places like the fort were a hazard for me most times, too many ghosts. I kept my walls up as much as I could but one snuck through.

We were standing in the middle of the fort, on the green surrounded by the high walls. I felt a prickling sensation and turned to look. Up on the wall, staring out at the sea, stood an officer of the Confederate Army. He was still as stone and I got the feeling he'd never stopped watching and guarding the grounds since the war. He lingered until right before I got back in the car and we continued on to Tybee Island. I understood how he felt about protecting his turf and his sense of duty. It's how I felt about my house.

The small community on Tybee Island sat on the edge of the ocean, nestled among the marshes. Mama and Daddy used to bring me out to see the baby turtles hatching right in the sandy beaches. We'd walk out on the long wooden pier and Daddy would try to catch fish. I held the memory close to my heart.

117

Hours passed as we explored the area hand in hand. The pier, the lighthouse, even the old museum all felt new to me when seeing them with Jason. He snapped a couple pictures of me and I hardly recognized the girl I saw when I held the camera and flipped through them.

It was one of the best days I could remember in a very long time.

The sun was sinking and the tide was going out as we walked through the surf away from the crowds. Everything else in the world felt so far away. All my problems, all the stress was a distant worry.

"What were your parents like?" Jason asked.

"They were wonderful. I used to think I was the luckiest girl alive. We did so much together. This was one of our favorite places to visit, actually. Mama was a historian so she filled my head with these amazing stories about the past."

"I think you get some of that from her."

"Thank you. Daddy was a big man. At least he felt that way to me. He was larger than life, ya know? He always had a smile on his face or a joke to tell. He lost a little of that spark when Mama died but he rarely let me see it. I still miss them both every day." I took a deep breath, not letting the sadness and shadows of the past intrude on today.

"I remember once we came out here to watch the turtles hatch. I must have been six or seven and we drove here in the morning because Mama had an event she was helping with for the Historical Society. We got to the beach across the island and the little turtles had just broken through their shells. They were so cute and tiny as they struggled up out of the nest and made their way to the beach. There was one egg though that didn't hatch and I wouldn't leave until it did. So we sat there all day and waited. Not long after the sun set, it broke open and the little guy made the trek to the water by himself. Mama missed the event she'd planned and never complained once. As a little girl I didn't think much of it but now I understand what that meant."

"You were lucky," Jason said as he squeezed my hand.

"Being here, I feel closer to them or if not them, at least closer to the memories of our family. What about your parents?"

He stared straight ahead. "I've had two sets of parents. The ones I had before Dylan died were amazing. Mom was involved in everything, drove us to every practice and game, baked cookies when we had friends over. My dad was the kind of father who'd take you out back and teach you how to throw a football or how to punch. We did a lot of camping and hiking and skiing. Our family was a unit. My friends joked about how we were one of those tight TV sitcom families. It made me feel good.

"After Dylan died, it all changed. They started disappearing. Their

118

forgiveness never felt complete and they looked right through me, like I wasn't there. Dylan died that day but so did our family. I knew I needed to get out of there as soon as I could so, I did. We still don't talk much."

I leaned my head on his shoulder and said, "I guess I'm not the only one who has had to live with ghosts."

"I never thought of it that way but you're right. Ghosts or zombies, my parents acted like the living dead. Neither one of them recovered. I miss having them in my life, but at the same time, I'm thankful I do have some wonderful memories. Maybe it will change someday. I keep telling myself that time heals but the longer it goes by, the more I consider myself an orphan."

"Have you told them this?"

He sighed heavily. "No, but I should. I love them with all my heart and want them to be there for me. I'll think about going to see them soon. If anything, I'll know I gave it my all."

We walked more in silence. It amazed me how similar we were. There probably weren't many people in Jason's life that he could really talk to.

Jason drew me down beside him as he sat in the sand and wrapped his arm around my shoulders.

It felt so right, sitting with him, watching the sun kiss the ocean and turn the sky a kaleidoscope of pinks, purples and oranges. I raised my camera and took a bunch of pictures as the fiery globe sank further and further into the horizon.

Finally, it disappeared and I sent out a little wish that the peace of this day would stick with me through what was to come.

Chapter Twenty-Seven

Something felt off in the house tonight.

I should have known the high of spending my day with Jason wouldn't last. The minute I stepped in the house I felt suffocated. Reminding myself it would all be over soon usually helped, but it didn't. Now I was worried about the house being too still and quiet.

As I walked up the huge staircase I couldn't help but be nervous. Catherine seemed to come at me when I least expected it or had my guard down. The closer my birthday got, the more time I spent looking over my shoulder.

Near Marietta's room I heard voices.

The door was partly closed but no light came from inside. I paused to listen. Cold air drifted out of the room so I knew Catherine was in there as well. Standing as still as I could, I strained to hear what they were saying.

"Why can't you leave me alone?"

It was Marietta. Her voice sounded hoarse and pleading, beaten down. It pulled at something inside of me. I wanted to rush in and help. I imagined her huddled in the dark talking to shadows, sort of like Gollum in Lord of the Rings.

I never imagined the shadows would talk back to her.

"We're not done yet."

Catherine. I knew her voice as if it was my own. It was dainty, feminine, and accented strongly. The echo beneath it chilled me every time she spoke. It was dark and sinister, a complete contrast to the soft Southern voice. It gave the voice depth, making it come alive.

Marietta whimpered and said, "I've done everything you asked of me."

I leaned closer. How Marietta ended up with Catherine inside her and controlling her was one mystery I needed to solve.

"Yes, you have." The voice drawled out, as if contemplating the answer.

"I've been pleased with your cooperation. I can feel myself getting stronger every day. Soon I'll be able to complete my plan."

"Then, please, let me go. You promised..."

Catherine snarled, "I'm well aware of what I promised but you're stuck with me until I've taken care of that sad little stepdaughter of yours. She has something I want."

Marietta started crying in earnest now, loud sobs that made me want to cover my ears. I forced myself to stay still though. I needed to find out what Catherine had in store for me. What could I possibly have? Absently, my hand reached for the necklace I still wore. No, she wanted me dead long before Margaret gave it to me.

"I never wanted to hurt Quinn. Everything you do to her, I feel it. You make me feel it."

One of my earliest memories of Marietta swam to the surface of my thoughts. Not long after marrying Daddy and moving into the house, she took me shopping for back-to-school clothes. I remember being excited and nervous. Marietta was such a well put-together woman and I was an awkward teenager. I wanted some of her poise to rub off on me.

We had lunch, shopped and talked. It was like having a mama again. I was a flower starved for the sun. At the time, I saw it as a bright beginning and it was.

At least it was for a while.

The voice laughed. "You will do as I say until I'm through with you. Don't worry. It won't be much longer. I'll have my revenge and the life I deserve and you'll be free of me."

I listened as Marietta continued to sob while the air grew colder. If I'd been paying attention it would have clued me in to the fact that Catherine was coming closer.

Suddenly, the door slammed open and I was face to face with a dark, towering mass. I braced for pain but all I felt was her presence in my head.

Eavesdropping is not very ladylike.

I backed up to the other side of the hall until I couldn't go any farther. The shadow pressed close, enfolding me and I gagged on the smell.

Don't have anything to say now?

Wanting to show her I was strong, I spoke instead of thinking my words. "I have plenty to say to you. Go away and leave me and my family alone."

Your family? That's an interesting choice of words. They don't want you, they never did. I've been inside Marietta's head long enough to know she can't stand the sight of you.

"Marietta treats me bad because you force her to. I heard you just now.

She wasn't like that until you possessed her. Why can't you move on and get over it?"

You think I want to be stuck here? In this horrible period? I would love to be somewhere else, some place where memories of the past won't assault me. Do you think I enjoy being stuck in this house with Jackson? He's a constant reminder of everything I lost, my dreams, my future, my soul.

"All you have to do is let go, Catherine. Let go and all of your pain will be gone. You don't have to hurt me the way you were hurt."

I will never let go of my dreams. You're an important part of that, Quinn.

All the fear and uncertainty welled up at that moment and I brought myself to a new low.

"Do you want me to beg, Catherine?" Even to myself I sounded hysterical. "I will. If you want me to get on my knees and beg you to let me live, I will. Please, don't do this. Don't do to me what William did to you. I've never done anything to you! Please, leave me alone."

The shadow stilled momentarily and I wondered if my words penetrated into any humane part of Catherine that still existed. As the seconds dragged on and on I began to hope.

But the hope was shattered when Catherine advanced on me with renewed force. Again, I expected pain but got none.

When I first realized I was dead, the need for revenge filled me up until I wasn't myself anymore. It feeds me and gives me power. Year by year that need for revenge grows. It consumes me and licks at my skin every hour of the day. I can't let it go because without it, I won't exist. Imagine being in excruciating pain every second. Exacting my revenge is the only thing that will make it go away. If I do this, the darkness goes away.

Her words terrified me. They were so malicious and focused. That crazy voice in my head craved revenge, like it was a drug. Getting Catherine to give up the power her quest for revenge fueled would not be easy.

Some part of me still thought I could reason with her.

"You do realize, don't you, that once you get rid of me, your vengeance will be over? When I'm gone, who will you focus those feelings on? Everything that you've been obsessing about for years will be over. What will you do then, Catherine?"

She leaned forward and a tendril of shadow reached out in the shape of a hand. I tracked it as it came closer but had nowhere to run; I was trapped. The hand reached up and stroked the side of my face, tracing down the jawbone to my chin. The touch was light and extremely cold almost numbing my entire face.

Then, to my shock the hand grew solid. I felt the fingers clamp onto my chin and turn my head from side to side as if assessing me. My entire body shook in fear.

When you're gone, I'll have everything I ever wanted.

Chapter Twenty-Eight

I wasn't even sure why I was going to Baubles today to work. Yesterday resembled a dream and the quickest way to lose that light carefree feeling was to be around my family so I knew I should avoid them.

The thing was, any extended period of time I spent out of touch with them made me worry, especially about Marietta. I didn't want to lose sight of the light at the end of the tunnel.

When you're gone, I'll have everything I ever wanted.

Those were Catherine's words and they both confused and scared the crap out of me. What could she possibly mean? I had no possible idea what she really wanted from me.

Walking in, I waved to the other hairdressers as I went to the back of the salon. As usual these days, Marietta was nowhere around. The bathrooms were probably dirty. If I didn't clean them, they wouldn't get done. Before I could grab the mop and bucket of cleaning supplies, my gaze drew to the 'pageant' room. The door stood halfway open but something wasn't right.

I reached in to flip on the light. When it came on all I could do was stare in horror.

"Oh no," I said in a breathless voice.

Every dress was shredded into hundreds of pieces. Satin and tulle were flung across the room. Ragged pieces of lace and other materials littered the floor. I'd never seen such destruction. It was like a wild animal had been let loose in here. Nothing was left untouched. Even Marietta's industrial sewing machine was in pieces.

I was torn. I wanted to go inside the room and try to figure out what happened. On the other hand, if I were in that room when someone else came in, I'd look guilty.

And that's exactly what happened.

Marietta, Anna and Suzie picked that exact moment to walk in the back door. I turned towards them and watched the various reactions play across their faces.

Anna looked relieved. I remembered her telling me about how she did the pageants only to please her mom and sister. I had the fleeting thought she did it until I looked at her mama.

Marietta's reaction didn't surprise me. In fact it made a sick kind of sense. Smug satisfaction settled into her features before she caught me looking. In the blink of an eye, she changed her look to one of outrage.

It was Suzie's reaction I had no time to prepare for.

"You witch!" She yelled and came at me with everything she had. I felt her hands grab onto my hair and her nails scratch down my cheek and neck. All of her strength went into her fists as they pummeled me. I tried to cover myself as best I could but I felt a few connect. "Why do you always ruin things?"

Deep down, I knew this was exactly the reaction Catherine was looking for. In her eyes it was one more way to beat me down.

I tried pushing Suzie away from me but she had a death grip on my hair. Finally, I felt someone tugging her away from me as a tearing sensation prickled my scalp.

When I was able to straighten up and open my eyes, I saw Anna holding her back. Suzie clutched a clump of dark brown hair. I held my hand up to my head where it throbbed like crazy.

I was ticked off. "I didn't do this Suzie! I just got here."

She didn't believe me and kept struggling against Anna. "You expect me to believe that? You disappear yesterday and here you are, caught in the act. Mom, do something!"

Marietta was standing off to the side watching but at her daughter's words she stepped forward and slapped me across the cheek—hard.

It completely stunned me.

I think it stunned the girls, too, because Suzie froze and Anna gasped. Once I had a chance to get over the shock, I gathered myself up and pointed at Marietta.

"She's the one who did it. She did it knowing I would be blamed." Even as I said the words I knew how stupid they sounded. It wouldn't mean anything without proof.

"Don't you dare try to pin this on my mom. You're a sick freak!"

Marietta's bizarre behavior continued as she calmly said, "Just get it cleaned up."

Her voice was calm. Nothing like I'd imagine the real Marietta would react. A pageant mom would have freaked out. She turned and walked into the front of the salon.

Suzie stared after her spellbound, as if she didn't even recognize her. I wondered if she would finally see that her mom wasn't acting normal. She turned back to me with hate in her eyes.

"Of all the things you've ever done, this is the worst. I'm going to make sure you are *ruined.* I'll never forget what you've done."

"What if it isn't Quinn's fault, Suzie?" Anna whispered almost too quietly to hear. I understood why, too. It wasn't often she went up against her twin. "What if she's right and mom did it? You saw how she acted just now. She didn't even care."

Suzie spun, causing Anna to flinch.

"You're starting to sound as crazy as her," she pointed back at me. "If I didn't know better I'd think you were taking her side. Our pageant dresses are ruined."

Anna was a deer caught in headlights. Her huge eyes filled with fear and sadness. "I'm not taking anyone's side. Mom has been acting weird."

"I think you're seeing things. Maybe you're seeing things the witch wants you to see. She wants us all destroyed. She's jealous."

I knew the best thing I could do was keep my mouth shut. I didn't want to. The way Suzie was laying into Anna bothered me. Why couldn't she see what was going right in front of her? She must be more self-absorbed than I thought.

Suzie flipped her hair and flounced off in the direction her mama had gone. She turned back to Anna. "Coming?"

Anna nodded and followed her out. Just before she was out of sight, Anna turned back and gave me a sad smile. Then she mouthed the words, 'I know it wasn't you.'

I wasn't sure whether to feel relief or surprise that she believed me. Considering she came to me about Marietta's behavior, I wanted to hold her words close. The fact she knew it wasn't me meant the world.

Suddenly, the events of the past few minutes came crashing down, mostly from the pain on my scalp and my face. Suzie fought like a girl, but it still hurt. I rubbed my stinging cheek where Marietta had slapped it.

I had to get out of there.

I darted to the back door, taking one last look over my shoulder at the destroyed dresses. Most of them had been ridiculously cheesy but still beautiful. A lot of time and care went into making them. The mess reminded me of what my life felt like lately.

Chasing the thought away, I left the salon in search of the light, careless feeling I knew I would lose if I was around my family.

I hoped I could find it again.

Chapter Twenty-Nine

The day dragged on endlessly. Jason and Abby were both working so I wandered around town with no destination in mind. I put off going home until the last possible minute. The less time I spent with Catherine, the better.

I wanted to take some time tonight to try to speak to Margaret. Since the ball I'd felt her presence, but had not spoken with her again. Finding out about my family, and if anyone else had been harassed by Catherine through the years, was a priority. It would give us a better idea of her motivations.

At least that's what Travis said. And I wanted to have something to tell him tomorrow.

I turned off all the lights in the attic except one and sat in the middle of the bed. Taking a deep breath I asked, "Margaret? Are you here?"

Silence stretched as I listened. Nothing.

"Please, I need your help. You've been there for me all this time. I have more questions."

The longer I waited the more I thought nothing would happen. The house was still. I faintly sensed Jackson downstairs but that was it.

I wasn't sure how long I sat there but eventually I grew tired. Just as I was turning to lie down, I felt her materialize in the room.

Same as before, she appeared startlingly solid and real.

"Hello Quinn," she greeted as she sat beside me. "What can I help you with, dear?"

Now that she was here, I had no clue where to start and was suddenly nervous talking to her about Catherine in the house. I heard Marietta come home earlier so I didn't want to do anything to get her attention.

"Can we talk about Catherine? I mean, can she hear us?"

Margaret cocked her head to the side, listening or concentrating. For a moment an irrational fear hit me that maybe it was another one of Catherine's mind games. Maybe she was pretending to be her mother. Then, the feeling I normally developed around Margaret settled over me and chased the thought away.

"I think we're safe for now. She doesn't seem to be aware of my presence up here."

"So you can all sense each other, you and Catherine and Jackson? Isn't that awkward?" Ever since the incident in the dining room, I'd been curious as to how Catherine and Jackson could exist in the same house all these years and not have any resolution.

"We are but not in the way you're imagining. Each of us is here for a reason; whether it's because we can't let go, like Jackson or because we're trying to atone for something horrible we did, like me. We're not roommates. Each of us exists in our own bubble so to speak. When I pass Jackson on the stairway I'm aware of him, but I have no need to interact with him."

Thinking of Jackson waiting for Catherine made me sad. "Why won't he just leave, move on? It's so sad."

Margaret shook her head and said, "I think he likes being near her. He remembers who she was, the girl he fell in love with, and hopes that one day she will be that girl again. He's going to be waiting a long time."

"How long has she been in this house?"

"I don't rightly know, sweetheart. I don't think she was able to remain here until your stepmother came along."

"That doesn't make sense though and it's something I wanted to ask you. Why, Marietta?"

"I wish I knew. Your stepmother allowed her to come into her body and into this house. That is all I've been able to learn. Catherine saw an opportunity and took it."

It was the same thing Travis mentioned but it still didn't add up. Marietta always appeared to be a smart woman, not the kind who would forge some kind of agreement with a ghost.

"So Catherine hasn't been here all along like, George, and Jackson?"

"No. She's tried to force herself in with other members of our family, but she was never strong enough. In your stepmother she found a willing host. In all the years she's been trying, she couldn't find a person weak enough to allow her in. She must have come to Marietta at a very vulnerable time. Forcing herself on someone could, and has, had disastrous results."

The hair on my neck prickled. "What do you mean by disastrous results?"

Margaret was quiet for a minute or so and I got the feeling she was hesitant to tell me something. Whatever it was, I knew I wouldn't like it.

"Catherine has presented herself to others before and tried to gain control of them. A couple of those times have resulted in the unexpected death of her intended host."

I felt my eyes widen. "What do you mean by unexpected death?"

My breathing picked up. Right when I thought I knew as much as I needed to about Catherine, it got worse. The hesitation on Margaret's face made me want to shake her and force her to say the thing she was holding back. Finally she spoke and my world came crashing down.

"I mean the person appeared to be in perfect health before they died. Not every death was her fault but some were."

She said the words so slowly and so carefully. The second the meaning of her words hit me, I almost got sick.

"Mama? Daddy?" I shook my head back and forth, trying to dislodge the possibility from my mind. It was too horrible to even imagine.

Margaret reached out and laid a cold hand on my arm. Normally, her touch or presence calmed me. I didn't even notice it right now.

"Not your father but I've always suspected Catherine's involvement with your mother's passing. Diane was in perfect health, in the prime of her life. In the weeks and days leading up to her death, I felt Catherine around the house. It doesn't mean anything but I've always wondered if it was more than coincidence."

I expected tears to come but all I felt was a rush of anger. Looking back, I couldn't remember anything about Mama's behavior that would have hinted she was being bothered by a ruthless spirit. Of course I was a child then, what did I know?

Other than anger, all I felt was a spreading numbness and sense of defeat. I realized how fruitless I was in thinking I could possibly stop Catherine. She was more powerful and evil than I ever knew.

"I didn't tell you this Quinn so you would shut down. I told you this so you would fight. If I'm right, she took something very special from you. Catherine deprived you of a mother. You can't let her get away with it again."

"But what's different now?" I asked sullenly. "What makes this time any different from the others? I'm nothing special. She's made sure of that from the beginning. Plus, she's even more powerful now."

"The difference is that now you're aware of her. You know what she's up to and where she is. You know her weaknesses. That will be the key."

I wasn't sure I believed her. Realizing Catherine might have had something to do with Mama's death cut me to the bone. My heart ached and my chest burned in rage. I wished I had an outlet for it. It's not something I'd ever experienced before and I couldn't focus. Logically, I knew I needed to keep a cool head and not lose sight of our goal; to get rid of Catherine once and for all.

That would be the best revenge possible.

I was terrified of how I would react next time I saw her, though.

"How do I keep this all in, Margaret?"

"Oh sweet child, the smartest thing you can do is lock away the pain and anger you're feeling right now. We're not even certain it's true. It's always been a suspicion. If you let those feelings interfere, you might lose everything. If you give in to them, you give in to her."

She was right. "I'll try as hard as I can to not let it slip. I don't even think I can tell Jason. It'll scare him and he'll try all over again to change my mind about going up against Catherine. There is no way I'm backing down now."

Her cold hand touched my cheek and turned me to face her. "I agree you shouldn't tell him yet. But don't close yourself off to him, baby. He is your future."

If I even have one, I added silently.

Chapter Thirty

The next morning I met Jason and Travis at a small diner for breakfast.

I felt incredibly out of it today. The revelations from Margaret last night bounced around in my head. I knew I shouldn't think about Catherine's possible involvement in Mama's death. A brain aneurism is a quick and often unexpected way to die but that didn't mean anyone caused it. The image of Mama crying out in pain as a dark shadow tried to force its way into her body kept flashing in front of my eyes.

Locking it up, as Margaret told me to, was one of the hardest things I've ever done.

Jason, complete in his disguise, arrived first and sat down beside me. He gave me a quick kiss and pulled out the menu.

"How are you? How have things been since I called yesterday afternoon?"

Clamping down the urge to cry on his shoulder about Mama, I sipped my juice before saying, "It's been interesting. I'll wait and fill you and Travis in at the same time."

We ordered breakfast as Travis came in and sat down. Again I wondered if we were right to be laying something this dangerous at the feet of someone so young.

After the preliminary greetings and Travis ordering pancakes, I fill the guys in on the events of the last couple days, leaving out anything to do with Mama. When I was done, Travis was the first to speak.

"So she's tried this before but never succeeded. It's because she has a human host now that she's so strong."

"I don't understand how that makes her strong." Jason said as the waitress delivered our food.

"An entity has to draw its power from a source. Many paranormal investigators believe ghosts are forms of energy. In order to manifest and manipulate things they need to take energy from whatever is around them. They can take it from the air, which results in cold spots. The air cools as energy, or heat, is taken from it. It's a sure sign an entity is nearby. Often on investigations we'll experience battery drain on all our electrical equipment. It's the same thing. They take the energy coming from those instruments."

"Some investigators have even started using pumps to supply the energy for the ghosts. This pump will give off bursts of electromagnetic energy in order to help something manifest," I added.

Travis flashed an impressed smile in my direction. "Exactly. So now, we can go one step further. What is the human brain but one big superconductor? The amount of electric charge put off by the human brain is staggering. It's a perfect source of power to draw from. That's what I believe Catherine is doing and why your stepmother is getting weaker and weaker. Catherine's taking a lot of energy to do these things. Emotion is a powerful tool."

I'd never thought of it that way before. Marietta's brain was probably an all-you-can-eat buffet to Catherine. It was a very disturbing thought.

"What happens if Catherine drains too much energy from her?"

"Then she'll keep growing weaker until her body can't handle it anymore," Travis answered. "But that won't happen. Somewhere, deep inside, Marietta still has free will. She can force Catherine out. We only have to figure out what will make Marietta come back to herself."

He gave me a perfect opportunity to bring up Anna.

"I think I have an idea about that. Her daughter, Anna, has noticed what's happening. She's even seen Catherine's shadow hovering behind her mom. If we bring her with us, she might be able to get through to Marietta. More than anything, Marietta loves her girls."

Jason stared at me hard. "Are you sure we can trust her?"

I nodded.

"That might be a good idea. We needed something that would jolt Marietta and using her daughter might be the edge we've been looking for. I'll want to meet her first and make sure she's absolutely aware of what we're attempting to do." .

"No problem, I can set that up." My birthday was in a few days so I needed to make sure it was soon.

During the rest of the meal we talked about that night and Travis shared more of his thoughts. My job was to keep Catherine focused on me. If she had her sights set on me, they had the opportunity they needed to deal with Marietta.

Travis said goodbye after we walked out into the heat of the day. He had a good plan and it calmed my nerves some. For a while it kept me distracted.

132

Jason swung his arm around my shoulders, chasing away the dark thoughts crowding in. "Look, I have to run but I want you to come by the hotel later." I looked up at him. "I've told you about what I sense in my room and I want to see if you do too. It might help keep your mind off things."

From any other guy, this would have made me suspicious. Inviting the local girl back to the hotel room was a line I bet a lot of actors or other guys used. Jason wasn't like that.

"Sure, I don't mind. When do you want me to come?"

"How about seven? Do you think you'll be able to get away?"

"I think so. She lets me have more free time now. It makes me nervous, but I still take advantage of it. She's not paying attention to much lately. Either way, I'll be there."

He stepped back and put his hands in his pockets. "You have no idea how much better I feel when you're not there."

Hearing his concern made me decide against telling him about what happened in the dining room. He was having a hard time not rushing in and being the savior. I could tell he was the type and maybe once this was all over, I'd let him do it occasionally.

Jason kissed me goodbye and left with Isaac. I watched him walk away and felt Margaret beside me, a cooling presence that I almost leaned into.

He's a wonderful boy. Always remember that, Quinn.

It was nice to get away from the house that night. I spent the entire time avoiding Anna or even looking at her. I was afraid that if I did, I wouldn't be able to keep my mouth shut. Even with all their good looks and popularity, I never envied Anna and Suzie because I knew they were pitiful.

When I left the kitchen, I heard Suzie whining about how much time I'd been gone lately, and how I didn't do as much housework as I used to. Marietta's reply was ice in my veins.

"Don't worry, sweetie. She won't be here much longer."

I walked outside and instantly the stress and the frayed nerves abandoned me. Not even my beloved house comforted me the way it used to.

The hotel Jason was staying at was located in the Riverfront district, an old hotel with a lot of character. Dwelling on the fact that I would be in Jason's room with him, alone, made my stomach roll in slow, lazy turns.

I walked through the lobby knowing I looked guilty. I worried my face was an open book screaming out the fact that I was going up to Jason Preston's room. He told me the security was pretty lax which surprised me. After all, he was a big movie star. I figured girls would be clamoring to get up to his room and take a peek at him.

I passed Isaac as I stepped off the elevator. He stood stationed at the end of the hall between the elevators and the door to the stairway. No one would be able to get past him.

"Hey Quinn," he greeted with a wink. I lifted a hand in reply since my mouth was too dry to speak.

Before I knocked on Jason's door I sucked in a large gulp of air as I lectured myself for making a bigger deal out of this than it actually was.

He opened the door with a huge smile but blocked me from coming in. "I've got something to show you and I can't wait for you to see it."

I noticed then that he was bouncing in place like a little kid.

Curiosity got the best of me. "Well, can I come in?"

He snuck a glance behind him but didn't move. "Close your eyes."

I did as I was told while he took me by the hand and led me forward into his room. Reaching out with all my senses, I tried to pick up hints of what he was up to.

"Okay, you can open them."

Jason's entire suite had been transformed into a mixture of a Christmas wonderland and a child's birthday party. A small, lighted tree stood on the table in the corner, decorated with lights and ornaments. There were even presents under it. Christmas lights were strung around his window and a big, stuffed snowman sat in the desk chair. Across the wall hung a 'Happy Birthday' banner and balloons of all shapes and sizes floated in the room. To top it all off, a small round purple cake with candles on it sat beside the Christmas tree. It was the most beautiful and magical thing I'd ever seen.

"How did you do this?" I asked in wonder. I didn't trust myself to look at him yet so I kept my eyes trained on the little tree.

"It's amazing what you can get when you've been on TV or in a movie or two."

He sounded a little embarrassed so I gave him a playful shove.

No one had ever done anything this special for me. Christmas and my birthday were always days I tended to avoid. I recalled telling him about how I hadn't really had Christmas or birthdays and how much I missed it.

"I can't believe you remembered."

He walked over and kissed me lightly.

"You deserve a little light in your life, Quinn." He brushed the hair out of my eyes. "When you told me about missing the holidays and how your parents were so into them, I started thinking about doing something like this. It's silly and I kept second guessing myself. I hope you don't mind."

I sucked in my breath. "This is...I've never... I don't know what to say."

Never had I seen him look so nervous and unsure of himself. Instead of answering, he reached over and picked up one of the presents under the tree.

"Open it," he said. And the grin was back, showing me his perfect teeth.

In five years, the only Christmas presents I'd opened were from Abby and her mama. My memories of loud, busy mornings opening presents were part of another lifetime. Honestly, giving me even a fraction of the feeling I got those mornings with my parents was the only gift I needed.

I took the present gently from him and memorized every single detail. The shiny red paper had glittery snowflakes on it, wrapped in a bright green ribbon.

Giving him a hesitant smile, I ripped it open.

"I hope that's the right kind, I had to ask Abby what camera you had."

Inside the box was a large zoom lens and it was top of the line. I knew because I often gazed longingly at it in the camera shop.

I set it down on the table and threw my arms around him.

"You have no idea how much this means to me," I whispered in his ear.

While his arms cradled me I felt safe, protected. Something I hadn't felt in a long time. Then I thought about him leaving and I remembered the loneliness from before. A dull ache spread through my chest. In that moment, I knew I was falling for Jason. And that scared me more than anything Catherine had planned for me.

Chapter Thirty-One

Later that night, I walked out of the bathroom towards the attic stairs, still buzzed from my time with Jason. I could find no words to describe how I felt about what he did for me. Well, that was a lie. I knew the word I would use to express my feelings towards him but I didn't think I could ever bring myself to use it. It was *way* too soon.

My foot had just hit the bottom step when something stopped me. Of course, I knew what it was right away. I didn't see Marietta. All I saw was a growing shadow advancing down the hallway. Running was pointless so I pressed myself up against the wall and hoped it would pass by. Like that would ever happen. I was getting attacked almost every night now.

The icy cold hit me first, knocking the wind out of me. The fierceness of the cold always surprised me, that startling realization that something could be so cold it hurt.

My instinct was to scream but as I opened my mouth, the cold surged down my throat and stole my breath. It wasn't the choking or suffocating on dirt like before. This was invading and reaching into every inch of my body. It felt as if something was pouring all the darkness and coldness in the world straight into my soul.

And same as before, I was powerless to stop it. I couldn't make a sound.

Then, my feet lifted off the floor into mid-air before I slammed into the wall behind me. The only thing I could see was blackness. It moved as if it were alive, shapes came in and out of focus; shapes of things that could only existed in nightmares.

I vaguely heard the thought 'why' run through my mind and was shocked when I got an answer.

"You know."

Staring into the void in front of me, I was even more afraid. Something about that voice made me want to curl up and hide every single time it invaded my mind.

Please, I thought desperately.

A deep, menacing laugh echoed through my head. If I hadn't frozen already from whatever was taking over my body, that voice would have done the trick.

What do you want from me?

No matter how many times I asked that question, I still hoped for a response. I hated that I sounded so weak and wished I could fight back. Before when she attacked me, I often felt myself fading. Now I was extremely aware of every sensation going on in my body.

"You're the last Roberts." The voice surrounded me and pressed in from all sides. It was impossible to tell which direction it came from. "I want to make sure it stays that way."

It won't work.

Something changed. Whatever control this mass had been exhibiting suddenly vanished and my suspended body quivered with the anger that blasted me. I was lost in a raging ocean, fueled by a hurricane of anger, helplessly bounced around and threatening to be swept away.

"You're a stupid girl to doubt me." It roared, blasting into all the corners of my mind.

You can't hurt me.

I knew the minute I thought it I'd made a mistake. Who was I to try to bluff something I didn't understand? It had already hurt me, even tried to kill me but I wasn't prepared for what happened next.

Thousands of pinpricks pierced me from the inside and out. The pain was so intense that for a moment I couldn't think of anything else. I became a living, breathing object of pain. It scared me more than anything else I'd seen or experienced up until that moment.

That fear caused me to fight back with everything I had. Unfortunately, all I had were my thoughts and my feelings. I thought of my parents and my love for them, flashing through my most cherished memories and pushing them out into the darkness. Memories like walking down the riverfront hand in hand with Mama and Daddy or sitting in the kitchen watching Mama make pancakes for breakfast or them tucking me into bed at night.

At first, I didn't think it made a difference but slowly I sensed the hold over me lessening and the darkness growing smaller. Finally, I was free and dropped to the floor in a pile. Strange enough, when I looked down at my arms and legs, hundreds of pin-sized dots of blood lined them.

I ran my hand over my arm in a daze, spreading the blood in a thin film. My head spun and I blacked out.

A scream brought me back and I had no clue how long I'd been unconscious. I noticed Suzie looking down at me in horror. Following her gaze, I saw my body still covered in blood.

"What did you do, freak?" Suzie demanded. I glanced up at her, tearing myself from the sight of the blood. She looked torn between disgust and concern. "Is that your blood?"

I shook my head, "I think so."

Now she gave me a confused glare. "If you're not wounded it can't be your blood. I bet its pig blood and you're doing some ritual. What is it for this time? To make something happen to me or my sister? Its payment for what happened to the dresses, isn't it?"

She walked up and got in my face. I didn't even have a chance to reply to her ridiculous notion.

"I told you once before, this isn't over," she promised before she stomped off down the hall.

I couldn't believe how incredibly stupid and paranoid she was. What if I'd actually been hurt?

Slowly, I got to my feet. I was still shaky and almost crawled to the bathroom. More than anything, I needed to wash the blood off me so I could feel normal again.

As the water beat down on me I wondered how it would end. The thought of this ending in my death, sent my body into convulsions. It terrified me and I didn't see how it was fair that I should have to pay for the mistakes of my ancestors. I was sick of waiting but terrified to do anything about it.

No matter how much I loved the house and living in Savannah, my life was more important. I wanted a future, a family. I wanted everything that I'd missed out on.

I needed to leave.

The thought made me double over in pain. Everything I had left existed in the very boards of this house. The idea of walking away from it seemed extreme but I knew I could do it. All I needed to do was wait for my birthday and my trust fund. I'd be able to go anywhere in the world.

The idea intrigued me. I could travel the world with just my camera and a backpack. The freedom that required pulled at me in a way I never thought it would. It almost made the pain of leaving a tiny bit more bearable.

Could I do it?

I had to do it. For my safety and even the safety of those I cared for. I stepped out of the shower and realized that if I left, it just might help Marietta too. Without me, she could sell the house and maybe Catherine would leave her alone. I'd even sign the house over to her if it meant this would all end.

Finally, after what felt like hours, I made it up the stairs. The room seemed safe, full of light and hope. It made me wonder which of the house spirits was present or if it was merely my imagination. Maybe the rest of the house had been overtaken by Catherine and her spirit had left my attic alone.

Exhausted, I fell into bed and directly into sleep.

Chapter Thirty-Two

"We're going to the club for dinner," Marietta told me as she ushered the twins out the door. Quiet enough so only I could hear, she said, "If I find out you left this house, you'll be sorry. I think we're both aware how capable I am." She smirked and closed the door behind her.

I didn't plan to go anywhere. Jason was filming and Abby working her new job. With a night all to myself, I had no clue what I would do.

As I walked up the stairs I passed Jackson in his usual spot, halfway up. It frustrated me that he was almost impossible to communicate with. Without looking directly at him I stopped and said, "You're really a pain, you know that?"

I felt him smile before I saw it spread across his handsome face.

"I wish I could talk to you. Why can't I talk to you?"

Sometimes the past is too painful to talk about.

Then, I watched his image grow stronger until he appeared mostly solid. I was nervous being this close to him. Catherine might still be sore that he'd come to my defense the other day and wouldn't like me talking to him. I decided it was worth the risk.

"I never got the chance to really thank you for what you did the other day."

She wasn't always so troubled. Catherine used to be full of life, a bright shining star I could never keep up with.

The last word I would have ever used to describe Catherine now was *troubled*. It made me sad to think of a man who seemed as strong and capable as Jackson still hung up on the same woman after a hundred and fifty years. Could love really be that overbearing? From what I'd seen of Jackson he didn't strike me as that guy, the guy who whined about a lost love.

"Why do you stick around for her? Did you love her that much?" Asking those things felt a little too personal but his answer was important to me for some reason.

Jackson looked up at the ceiling, mulling over what he would say. When he looked down at me I saw a grim resolution in his eyes.

I loved the vibrant young woman I fell instantly for. She was a drug to me until the day I left for the War. But that is not the reason I continue to stay. I stay because it's my fault she is like this.

Shaking my head slowly, I couldn't understand why he blamed himself unless there was more to the story than I knew.

"From everything I've heard, Jackson, you're not responsible for this. I'm not really sure anyone is."

You're wrong. When I came back home from the War I was different. It changes a man. The nightmares I saw, the nightmares I couldn't get rid of, left me in a place where I knew I wouldn't be able to give Catherine the happy ending she'd wanted. Don't get me wrong, I still wanted to marry her, but I needed time to heal first. Until the day I stepped foot back in Savannah I knew nothing of her marriage.

He paused and I watched him swallow hard as if the next part was difficult to talk about.

When I heard Catherine had married I was relieved. It's shameful to say but at least I knew I wouldn't have to explain to her why we couldn't marry and start a family right away. I loved her so much. I only wanted to be the man she remembered. Hearing she married a Yankee broke my heart but I wasn't going to screw things up for her.

I went to see her to say goodbye. It surprised me when she answered the door because I assumed they would have some house staff. Maybe Jennings didn't want any witnesses to the things he did to her. She looked as if she had fought a war of her own. Her face was bruised and her lip was cut. I saw death in her eyes, like she knew it was coming and she was waiting for it. She said she saw me come up the front walk and that she knew I'd always come back for her.

Catherine expected me to rescue her. Once she pulled me inside and told me all the horrible things that he had done to her, I had no choice. My first reaction was to hunt him down and kill him but she convinced me it would only land me in jail. We needed to run away. I didn't think twice about it and told her to meet me that night at the train station. I had money and we'd go to California where there was a fortune to be made. I remember her smiling and telling me she forgot what it felt like to smile.

That night I waited for hours and she never showed up. I worried that something might have happened to her so I went back to their house. No one was home. The next day as well, no one answered the door. By then I was in a fit not knowing where she was or if she was well. Later that week I found

Jennings having lunch with my father and some of his friends. A Southern gentleman would never come out and accuse anyone of anything unsightly in the presence of their equals and neither did I. I merely inquired as to her whereabouts, that I wanted to tell her I was home.

He looked me in the eye and told me she was with child and too ill to get out of bed. The men around the table congratulated him and ordered another round of drinks. It disgusted me. Not only was the man a monster, here was my father and other respectable members of the city buying him drinks. I had no reason not to believe him. To my battle weary mind, she had simply either decided to stay with him for the sake of the baby or fell too ill to meet me.

It wasn't until I had been in California for a few months that word of her disappearance finally reached me. I rushed home to Georgia but by then it was too late. William was missing and Catherine's family declared her dead. No one had any answers for me so I left Savannah for good.

I'm to blame because I can only guess he caught her sneaking out to meet me. Or he saw me leave the house. I'm to blame because I even went to see her in the first place. I'm to blame because it wasn't me who killed her murderer, even if it was after the fact.

The long speech drained Jackson's energy. His image faded until I almost didn't see him at all. It was an incredible story, tragic and romantic and doomed. My heart broke for him.

"I still don't understand how any of it is your fault. Even if you never went to see her, Jennings might have eventually killed her anyway. He was a nasty, violent man. No one could have known what went on behind the door of their home. You said it yourself, the War changed everything. Catherine was a victim of it as much as anyone. Her parents sold her to pay off their war debts. They are the ones she blames."

Jackson continued to fade and his voice came to me as almost a whisper.

Knowing and believing are two different things. I will do all I can to help you because I think it's why I'm here. Maybe I have a chance to redeem myself. I'll keep you safe, Quinn.

And I knew he would because that was the kind of man he was, a man who didn't shrink away from his duty.

"Does Catherine know you're here, in the house? Have you been able to apologize?"

Right before he faded away entirely I heard his soft reply.

The girl I loved is gone. That thing is not Catherine anymore and she never will be again.

Jackson disappeared. My heart ached for him and my mind spun. Nothing he had told me was tremendously significant but it filled in more of the blanks.

I was getting a better image of what Catherine's life, and death, was like. It wasn't pretty. A part of me pitied her but that felt dangerous.

The absolute worst thing I could do was let my guard down.

Chapter Thirty-Three

"Why are you so sure it's here?" Abby asked.

We were searching through Colonial Park Cemetery for Catherine's grave. Over the years, many of the burial records had been lost. I'd hoped the more direct 'look till you find it' approach would get us results.

Even after deciding I would be better off leaving, my conscience kicked in and I had reconsidered. My birthday was only two days away. Running away wouldn't solve anything. Marietta would still be possessed and I would lose any heritage I had left. Getting rid of Catherine was the only logical choice in my mind. Not that it made everyone happy but at least Abby and Jason were here with me tonight, hoping for a way to end it.

I looked around. "What I don't get is that it's dusk and it's so quiet. Normally this place is still crawling with tourists."

"Ah, that would be my fault," Jason answered from about ten feet away where he was studying a row of tombstones.

"What do you mean your fault?" I picked my way over to him. The dates on the tombstones appeared to be in the right time period. Maybe we were getting close. It had already been two hours.

He shrugged and I knew it meant he was trying to downplay something. "I made some calls, had it closed down for a few hours tonight. The city agreed to help me out."

Abby laughed. "Oh, so no big deal. You just asked them to keep everyone else out for a while? You know, sometimes, I think being a Hollywood actor has its benefits."

"Yeah, anytime you need to get into a cemetery at night, give me a call."

I listened to their banter with a smile on my face. They got along great and it was a weight off my shoulders. Abby and Jason were the two most important people in my life and I didn't know how I would have handled it if they weren't getting along.

Wandering a little farther from them, I entered a darkened part of the cemetery and pulled out my flashlight. Here, the tombstones weren't straight and neat, they leaned at all angles like crooked teeth. I sensed the spirits nearby but ignored them. I was here on a mission and nothing would distract me from it

I heard a slight breeze in the trees overhead as I tried to block out the spirit of a little girl begging me to help her find her mama. Her sad cries ripped me in two because she reminded me of myself. The lump in my throat grew as she came to stand right next to me. The sorrow pulsed off her and I fought to ignore her sweet little tear-streaked face.

She wore a lace and eyelet patterned nightgown that once upon a time must have been white. Now it was caked with dirt and grime, as was her face. The little girl's long blond hair rioted around her face in a clump of tangles.

Over and over she whimpered 'please' until it got to be too much.

Swallowing my tears I asked, "Where is she? Where is your mama?"

Instead of speaking, she lifted a filthy finger and pointed into a darker part of the cemetery. I was involved now, so I automatically reached out my hand to her. Coldness settled over my hand that led me to believe she was holding it. I should have been smarter but I followed her anyway, deeper into the cemetery, away from my friends.

Here, in the oldest part, the grave markers were nothing more than sagging stones. Any names or dates had eroded away by time and climate. The trees hung so low they blocked out any light and the moss hanging from them brushed my head and shoulders as I crept by. Only my flashlight gave off a meager amount of light.

But we were far from alone. Shadows stopped and watched us as we passed, some reached out their hands to touch me. These ghosts had been here longer than I could fathom. The depth of their sorrow and loneliness was almost too much to bear. I'd made a mistake.

I followed the girl past a tall, moss covered angel statue. Whatever grave it once marked had long ago been reclaimed by the trees. The angel itself was almost wrapped entirely in branches.

Finally, we stopped.

She walked forward slowly and knelt down in the grass. I took a few hesitant steps before being hit with a menacing presence. It scared me so much I didn't want to move. This wasn't Catherine. It was something different.

"What is that?" I quietly asked the girl.

She turned back to me with those huge sad eyes and said, "The bad man hurt my mommy and they made her sleep here in the ground. He hurt me too but I ran away. Now he stays here and keeps her from leaving."

"Can you leave?"

Tiny sobs came from her. "I don't want to leave my mommy."

I knelt down so that I was eye level with her, ignoring how the 'bad man' buffeted me with wind to keep me away. Reaching out with my senses, I tried to see if her mama was there but got nothing. Either her mama already passed on or she was hiding very well from the man.

An idea sprang to life inside me. I didn't know if it would work but I had to try. This little girl needed my help.

"Do you want to hear a secret?" Interest lit up her eyes and she nodded. "Okay, let's go back the other way and I'll tell you."

Once again, I felt the cold on my hand as I stood. I led her back past the angel into a less creepy part of the cemetery. As I hoped, the 'bad man' didn't follow.

I stopped and sat down on the dirty ground, patting the space beside me. The girl sat as well.

Please let this work.

"I'm going to tell you a secret. When they made your mommy lay in the ground, it wasn't her." She looked confused. "It was just her body. Everything that made your mommy special was in here," I touched my head, "and in here." I touched my heart. "When you mommy went to sleep in the ground, the best part of her went someplace special."

The little girl gasped in surprise. "Like Heaven?"

"Yes, like Heaven." I wasn't sure I believed in it but I wanted to use her beliefs to aid me. "You remember stories about Heaven, right? It's a magical place where you never cry and you can play with puppies all day long. And you get to eat anything you want."

I hoped it sounded like a magical place but seeing her smile light up her face, I knew I was on the right track.

"That's where your mommy went and I bet she misses you. You can go there, too."

"But I was bad and I lied," she whispered as her smile fell.

"You're sorry though, aren't you?" She nodded. "Then you can absolutely go. You want to see your mommy, right? All you have to do is close your eyes."

I watched her close her eyes while I tried to figure out the rest. This was the first time I'd ever tried to help a ghost. Part of me worried once I did, things would change dramatically for me but at this moment, I didn't care. This beautiful little girl shouldn't be left here all alone.

"Okay, I want you to picture your mommy in this place. Think about how much you want to see her and how much you love her. Think about how sorry you are for whatever bad thing you think you've done. Don't think about the 'bad man' or anything that would make you stay here."

At first, I didn't think it would work. Then I saw her image slowly start to fade. She continued to sit there with her eyes close and a smile on her face until she'd completely disappeared. I no longer felt any trace of her.

The joy that blossomed in my heart warmed me. Already I knew it wasn't something I wanted to do again. She reminded me so much of myself at that age, having just lost my own mama. I felt good about what I did.

Standing up, I made my way back to where I'd left off looking for Catherine's grave. I ran into Jason and Abby a few feet from the section where I would resume searching. They both looked panicked.

"Where did you go? We called for you," Abby demanded.

Jason watched me closely, but I kept my encounter with the girl to myself. It was too special to share.

"I was looking for the grave but I think all the stuff in that part of the cemetery is too old."

"We found it," Jason said as he pointed to the headstone. "I half expected something scary to pop out and grab me but it didn't."

"Yeah, he's kept a safe distance from it since we got here. He won't get any closer than this."

"I'm not as brave as you are, Abby. You've been stomping around on it."

I edged over and peered at the grave. "This is where it ends."

Jason texted Travis and told him to meet us here. While we waited the three of us stood there and stared at the harmless looking spot in the ground, each of us lost in our own thoughts.

Travis arrived a little while later. "So this is Catherine?"

"Yes."

He nodded his head and studied it.

Finally, he spoke, "I want to warn you that what you're asking me to do is dangerous. I want you to be aware of that from the start. There is a risk to your stepmother."

"I'm aware of that. I have to believe the risk is worth the reward."

I knew what Catherine was capable of when it came to her hosts, especially if she was responsible for killing Mama. The same thing wasn't going to happen to Marietta. I'd make sure of it.

"Okay," Travis began. "This is how it's going to happen."

We gathered around and listened to his plan.

Chapter Thirty-Four

Something woke me up.

It had taken me a long time to fall asleep. I kept thinking of the little girl in the cemetery and hoping desperately I'd been able to help her get to a much better place.

I shot out of the bed convinced it was Marietta standing vigil over me again. But I didn't see anything.

Then I heard a noise, whatever it was that woke me up, a clicking of something hard on a wood surface. It scratched and scraped and sent chills down my back.

Walking over to my desk I fumbled for the lamp and switched it on. At first the light was blinding but, as I got used to it, I scanned the room for something out of place. No stray shadows moved but I could not shake the forbidding feeling that seized me.

This time the noise was closer, off to my right.

I tried to follow it but didn't have very far to go. At the edge of my desk I caught sight of a movement the same time I heard the sound.

It was the necklace Margaret gave me.

Torn between curiosity and fear I watched as it inched slower and slower to the edge, as if it had a destination in mind. After a few more seconds, it stopped.

When I reached out my hand to touch it, it lifted up into the air. Startled, I jumped back and squealed. My heart was pounding in my chest. The pendant lay flat in midair with the chain dangling down behind it. If I didn't know better, I'd think I was dreaming

Not in this house, though.

Once more, it started to move. Inch by inch it floated closer to the window near my bed. I took a few slow steps behind it and jumped again when I heard

148

the pendant tap up against the glass. Even though it startled me, I sensed no danger from the necklace as I stepped up and wrapped my hand around it.

It was cold, which I expected, but it also hummed with some kind of energy. Then, I peered out the window, wondering where it could possibly have been headed.

I almost couldn't believe my eyes.

Instead of the back yard I was staring at a bedroom full of ornate furnishings, a fire in the hearth and a frantic Catherine packing a small valise.

She looked exactly as Jackson described. Bruises covered her face, her lip was cut and swollen. Her golden brown hair spilled halfway out of the combs trying to hold it up. The dress she wore was very plain and inexpensive looking. Remembering what Jackson said about their running away together, I imagined that she didn't want to stand out. That or her husband had beaten the desire to look beautiful out of her. I also noticed the necklace, the same one that drew me to the window, nestled in the neckline of her dress.

I realized I must be seeing the night she was supposed to meet him at the station, the night she died.

Suddenly, the bedroom door slammed open and a large man strode in the room. He had light blond hair receding at the forehead and cold scary eyes. Well over six feet tall, he was one of the biggest men I'd ever seen. He wasn't fat, just hard and lean. He radiated with a creepy vibe.

William Jennings.

Catherine clutched a pair of stockings to her chest as she whirled around, surprised by his sudden appearance. I saw the look of a trapped animal in her eyes. She knew what was about to happen. Even as an observer, I could feel the fear pulsing off her.

"What are you doing?" William asked. His voice was smooth and quiet, not what I expected from a man of his size. Still, it left me cold but with a hot prickling sensation on the back of my neck. He took another step towards Catherine.

Like a fish, she opened and closed her mouth trying to get air or words to form. William continued towards her, one slow agonizing step at a time. Catherine's eyes darted frantically, searching for any means of escape. There was none.

"I saw a man leave here this afternoon. Who was he?" Catherine shook her head, her eyes filled with panic. "I assume it was Jackson Merriwether. I heard he was back in town. What are you planning to do? Run away and meet him somewhere?"

Still Catherine was silent. I had a hard time relating the young woman I saw to the mean, violent spirit I knew. They were so completely different. This

Catherine I pitied.

"N-no, I wasn't g-going anywhere."

William silenced her with a backhanded slap that just about knocked her off her feet. She fell against the bed sobbing. I imagine the cries had more to do with her missed opportunity to escape than the humiliation and pain he caused, which she was probably used to.

I watched as he advanced towards her, grabbing her hair and standing over her.

"Why are you crying? Your place is here beside me! I will never let you go, do you hear me?"

He tipped her face up and thrust his fist down on it with a savage force. Sick to my stomach I watched him repeat the movement over and over until her beautiful face was nothing more than a bloody, oozing mess.

As quickly as he started, he stopped. William panted and tried to catch his breath. When he did, he glanced down and saw what he'd done.

In a move that sickened me even more, he knelt down and brushed the bloody strands of hair from her face. "I'm so sorry Catherine. It makes me mad to think of you leaving. Promise you'll never go. I love you so much. I need you."

His arms enfolded her tenderly and drew her close. The air whistled and gurgled out of her ruined nose. Her hands came up and I wondered both how she still had the strength to do it and how she could return his hug.

Only she didn't hug him back.

Catherine's shaking hands reached up to his neck where they squeezed.

"You can't hurt me anymore William. I never was yours." Her voice was weak and strained as she struggled to draw in air as well as squeeze the life out of him.

It must have taken William by surprise because it took a few seconds for him to react. And when he did it was more violent than what I'd already witnessed.

I couldn't watch.

Shutting my eyes tight I tried to block out the sounds of fighting and screaming. A snap echoed over to me, the sound of a bone being broken. I'd never heard anything like it in my entire life. Finally, there was a steady thumping sound and then silence. Well, silence except for the heavy ragged breaths of William.

He crouched over Catherine's broken body with his hands gathered in her hair. From the blood pouring out of her head I guessed the thumps were William driving her into the floor repeatedly.

Vomit rose in my throat but I couldn't tear my gaze away. Slowly, the scene in front of me faded, replaced by another.

I recognized the river but not the old wooden dock that jutted out into it. The night was quiet, accented only by the light of a half moon. William stumbled down the dock carrying a large sack over his shoulder.

Catherine.

He took one quick look around before tossing her body in the river as if it were nothing. Finally, the musty river scent I always smelled when Catherine was near made sense. That was where her body was tossed, nothing more than a piece of trash. As he watched it sink, he pulled the necklace out of his pocket and fingered it gently.

The scene faded once more and my normal backyard returned. I felt sweat cooling on my skin and bile still trying to force its way up my throat.

"What William didn't know is that I was still alive when he tossed me in the river."

I spun to find Catherine sitting on my bed, not as a shadow but as a form as real and solid as Margaret's. Her long dark hair curled past her shoulders softening her face even more. Her skin was flawless, almost like porcelain. I expected her eyes to be cold and flat but they weren't. I could see why, in her prime, Catherine had been the talk of the town.

My reaction surprised me. It wasn't the cold fear I normally felt around her presence, not after the horrific scene I just watched. I felt pity and sadness.

Pitying her was dangerous. I couldn't let myself forget what Margaret said about suspecting her involvement in my mama's death. The safest thing right now was to push that aside and concentrate.

She continued talking, "The potato sack he stuffed me in was tied up too tight. The minute I hit the water I tried to struggle but you saw what he did to me. I had no strength left."

Forcing myself to keep my guard up, I walked over to the desk and sat in the chair. This was a side of her I had no clue how to handle. Letting myself forget she'd tried to kill me multiple times was not an option.

"What happened to you was terrible, Catherine."

She daintily raised an eyebrow at me. "I didn't show you that so you would pity me. You wanted to know why I had a thirst for revenge and now you do."

Wanting to steer clear of the revenge aspect, I changed the subject. "How come you could move the necklace tonight? The other day when you tried, it sparked at you."

"Did you see me touch the necklace? Besides, who cares if I touch it or not, it's mine anyway."

"Margaret gave it to me," I said feebly. Now I'd have an entirely different attitude about wearing it knowing it was on her neck the night she died.

"It wasn't hers to give!" Catherine's voice turned vicious and her image faded as the dark shadow grew in response. Then, I watched as she gathered herself together and became solid once more.

"So how is this going to work? Your killing me?"

Her pretty face twisted into a smirk. "What makes you think I'll tell you?"

That was the problem. I had no clue. "We're family. Even as much as you hate our family, it should matter to you a little."

"It doesn't. You're confusing me with that pathetic thing you saw just now. I'll come for you, Quinn but I'll do it on my own power." She stood and stalked toward me. I fought the urge to run. "Not everyone gets their *happily ever after*."

Her words reminded me of Mama and I couldn't stop the words that came out of my mouth.

"Did you do something to my mama? Were you responsible for her death?"

At first, I didn't think she would answer me. Finally, she started laughing a cold, chilling laugh. "She was in the perfect position to help me get what I wanted. Unfortunately, she didn't see the benefit of working with me. I couldn't bend her to my will."

The truth hit me hard in the gut. Margaret was right. The anger I'd been carrying since she shared her suspicions with me faded to grief. I was breathless and lightheaded and the room spun. Vaguely, I was aware of shaking my head back and forth in a silent denial.

Before I could say anything to Catherine, she disappeared in the blink of an eye.

I remained alone with my tears, my pain and a renewed determination to beat Catherine and send her to Hell where she belonged.

Chapter Thirty-Five

Jason surprised me about mid-afternoon. I opened the front door to find him standing there, in his disguise, grinning at me. It didn't register at first to see him. I'd been in a daze ever since last night.

"What are you doing here?" I hissed, unsure why I kept my voice low.

"Don't freak out. I waited until everyone left." He walked in before I invited him.

"So, why are you here?" Jason glanced at me kind of funny, as if the question was rude and it hit me that it was. "I mean, I'm glad you came by. I didn't think we made plans is all," I trailed off.

"Are you already sick of me? I had the day off so I thought I'd see if you wanted to hang out or do some research." He shrugged. "If you have plans, I can go."

"No, Travis said to stay under the radar so that's what I'm doing. I can't bring myself to leave here yet."

Now that I knew the truth about Mama I wanted to spend the day making sure I was ready for Catherine tomorrow. Pretending it wasn't going to happen was too much to risk.

"You're thinking too hard," he observed.

"I have mixed emotions about what's going to happen tomorrow so I'm a little out of it. Unfortunately, I might not be the best company. Catherine showed me last night what Jennings did to her. I can't get it out of my head."

He took my hands in his. "You're scared; it's not lost on me. I want to be there for you, even if all I do is sit there and not say a word. Besides, I stuck it out through all your snarky attempts at playing hard to get. If I survived that, I can take on anything."

Before I could answer him, I heard a car door slam. I peeked out the window and saw Marietta coming up the walk.

"It's Marietta." I spun towards Jason. "You have to hide. Go up to the attic and please, *be quiet*."

He ran quickly up the stairs and I hurried into the kitchen, busying myself with the dishwasher.

When Marietta walked in, I tried hard not to make eye contact with her. I was convinced that after one look in my eyes, she'd know I was hiding something.

"What are you doing back so soon?" I hoped she didn't hear the tiny squeak in my voice.

Instead of answering me, she set down the local newspaper on the counter and pointed. I almost fainted.

On the front page of the *Lifestyles* section was a picture of me and Jason kissing on a park bench. Right next to it was one of us smiling for the cameras at the ball. How did they know it was the same person? I scanned the article below the picture.

"Seems as if Hollywood heartthrob Jason Preston has found a new love right here in Savannah. Her name is Quinn Roberts and she's the daughter of one of the city's oldest families. It all sounds like a match made in heaven but according to one of Roberts' stepsisters there may be more to the story. 'She practices black magic,' stated Suzanna Roberts. 'She's always doing things to us and terrorizing us at home. Quinn can make bad things happen and I often hear her chanting in a really, like, creepy language.' Suzanna adds, 'She always sneaks out to meet guys too. I think she puts spells on them or drugs them.' Is Quinn Roberts the same mystery girl we saw on Jason's arm at the Savannah Heritage Ball? Time will tell. Jason Preston is in town filming the movie adaptation of Black Night and has been linked to several up and coming actresses. The question remains, has Jason fallen for a hometown princess? Or has he been lured in by a teenage girl's Love Spell?"

"Well, well, I have to tell you, Quinn, I'm impressed you were able to snag a boy of Jason's caliber. Of course, keeping him is another story, one that won't have a happy ending." She looked me up and down with a sneer. "What would he ever see in you? I guess you can't really blame him. I'm sure you're giving him exactly what he wants."

I shook my head and opened my mouth but no words came out. The hurt and betrayal from Suzie's lies numbed me. She finally got her revenge for the destroyed dresses. Of all the things they had ever done to me, this was *the* worst. I'd never be able to show my face around town again.

Marietta must have taken my silence as an admission of sorts. She smiled smugly but it did nothing to improve her looks. She was so pale and withdrawn and withered, death was staring her in the face. Catherine was killing her. I took some reassurance that this was Marietta talking now, all on her own.

"Don't count on it lasting. You have absolutely nothing to offer him. Take a good look in the mirror." She paused. "I have the worst headache. It must be a migraine. I thought I'd take some of my pills and have a nap."

I watched her leave. Catherine seemed to linger behind, reaching towards me. I shrunk back against the counter but she slithered out, leaving the room bright again. As strange as it sounded, that didn't go nearly as bad as I'd imagined it would.

Sure, I was angry but it felt small compared to everything else going on.

Then panic welled up in me. I had to get Jason out of the house. The last thing I wanted was to cause him any harm. His being here with me could be a catalyst. I took the newspaper with me to show him, hoping it would convince him to get out of here.

Walking past Suzie's bedroom, I fought the urge to smash and rip and tear everything apart that she owned. The ticked off part of me wanted to get back at her but the cool, logical part said being happy with Jason would be payback enough.

I made my way up to the room as quiet as I could and found Jason sitting on my bed. He stood up as I came close.

"Everything okay?"

I handed him the paper and walked over to gaze out the window. Different emotions flitted across his face and I was relieved when the final one showed anger.

"I don't believe this. Who do they think they are? I can have my people release an actual statement. I'll make sure this is retracted and everyone knows the truth about us."

"Jason you don't have to do that. I mean, I'm upset, too, but it's not worth it. We have more important things to worry about in the next couple days."

"You are the most stubborn person I've ever met, do you know that? I'm not letting this go. We'll do it my way once your birthday has passed. I wish you'd budge on the little party we have planned tomorrow. I don't like it."

"Jason, you just don't get it. This thing has attacked me more than once and continues to hurt me. You're starting to sound like a broken record."

He looked sharply at me. "What do you mean *continues* to hurt you? You told me things have been quiet."

"They have, kind of. There were a couple incidents but I'm fine. I'm still here, aren't I? Did you ever stop to think that I'm just trying to protect you as much as you're trying to protect me? I don't want to be responsible if something happens to you. I can't live with that."

He silenced me with a kiss. Taken by surprise, I hesitated for a split second before finally sinking into it. It made me forget about everything else but him. I knew he'd freak out if I told him about the blood incident last night, so I didn't go into detail. No need to worry him any more that I already had. It was almost over.

My moment of nirvana came to an abrupt halt when I felt Jason being ripped away from me with savage force. I watched in horror as he slammed against the far wall and landed in a heap.

Catherine's presence exploded into the room, making it so dark that I couldn't see where Jason was. Like all the other times, I wasn't able to move. I never knew what to expect. Her attacks were never the same but this time I wasn't worried about myself.

"Jason!"

The darkness parted and I saw him standing there, his face twisted into fright. Then I watched in horror as a shadowy hand swiped across his body, leaving a bloody trail. There were now four long ragged wounds on his chest and one across his face. He didn't make a sound, only stared at me with horrified eyes.

I screamed and Catherine's laughter echoed back at me.

This time, the shadow went right through him. The large hole it left behind in his stomach oozed and dripped blood onto the floor of the attic. I tried to get to him but I couldn't get close enough.

I screamed hysterically as I watched him bleed to death. His eyes never left mine and the look on his face pleaded for me to help him. Slowly, his skin grew pale and grey. The light in his eyes faded. I was so scared and so ticked off.

"Your fight is with me Catherine. Leave him alone," I yelled.

I heard her in my head. *Always remember this is what I can do if you start thinking you can get rid of me*

Suddenly, she was gone. The light returned to the attic and my terror trickled away.

Jason got up off the floor where he first fell and sprinted over to me.

"Quinn, are you okay? I heard you screaming but I couldn't get to you."

Running my hands over his chest and face, I searched for the horrible wounds that I'd seen only seconds ago. There was nothing wrong with him.

It didn't make any sense. I saw him bleeding and dying. What was that? The thoughts jumbled in my head so I backed up and sat on the bed. Jason was still talking.

"I'm guessing that was Catherine." He turned my face towards him. "You are so pale. Please say something, Quinn."

"I saw you," my voice trembled, "she hurt you. And, and you were

156

bleeding."

The image popped back, vivid and frightening and I burst into tears. Jason wrapped me in his arms and rocked me. It was safe and comforting but my shaking didn't stop.

"Shhh, you're okay. I'm here and I'm okay."

I don't know how long we sat in that position but eventually I turned my face towards him and kissed him sweetly on the lips.

In a hush I said, "You have to go."

He stood up and put his hands on his hips. "I'm giving you two choices and you're not going to argue with me. You're leaving here with me now. I'll get you a room at the hotel. Or I'm staying here with you all night."

"You can't be serious."

Jason leaned down inches from my face. "I'm very serious, Quinn. Pick one."

The romantic part of me loved how he was trying to play the knight in shining armor. It made me want to swoon, like in an old fashioned movie. The stubborn side of me, the side that was independent and used to fighting her battles, got prickly.

"This is stupid, Jason."

He remained unmoving, giving me a hard stare.

"Fine. I'm not going anywhere. I won't run from it. This is my house. So, if you want to stay, stay. Don't say I didn't warn you. You have to keep yourself up here and stay quiet. Marietta would kill me if she found you in the house."

I briefly wondered if I meant that literally or figuratively. Marietta, the stepmother I originally cared about would 'kill' me in the sense that I'd be grounded for life. Marietta, under the influence of Catherine, was a whole other story.

It made me shudder.

"Okay, I'm glad that's settled." He kept the businesslike attitude but his eyes softened. "Don't worry. I understand what we're up against now. That scared the crap out of me. Once you walk out of here I'm going to curl up in a corner and start conversing with some higher powers."

He made me grin. Even though he joked, I saw the lingering fear on his face. All of a sudden I felt awkward. Where the heck was he going to sleep?

"I'll go get us some food."

Walking as softly as possible, I went downstairs. As I passed by Marietta's room, I noticed her laying there sleeping, unmoving. While Catherine terrorized me upstairs, Marietta must have slept through it. I wondered if she'd been aware of what happened. I remembered the day I heard her talking to Catherine about how she felt everything done to me. Did she feel it in her sleep as well?

To make it even stranger, I didn't sense Catherine anywhere around her, which meant she still roamed the house somewhere.

Luckily, I made it back up to the attic with my arms full of food without running into her.

I didn't like Jason being there. Not because I was nervous about being alone with him, that was certainly part of it. It was the vision Catherine showed me. I didn't want it to come true.

Later that night in Jason's arms, I listened to him breathing. In all the nights I spent in this room alone I'd never been as afraid as I was right now. Flashes from the vision Catherine forced me to see earlier kept playing across my mind. Afraid for Jason's life, I spent the night concentrating on the life-giving air flowing in and out of his lungs.

Chapter Thirty-Six

I woke up full of nervous energy.

Jason snuck out sometime in the early morning and I wouldn't be too far behind him. With all we had riding on today, I needed to stay as far away from Marietta and Catherine as possible.

Nothing could derail our plans. Today, everything changed.

A sickening feeling took root in my stomach as I gathered my things. If I ever set foot in this house again, especially with Catherine around, I would not survive it. My age and subsequent ownership of the house didn't magically negate the fact that Catherine wanted me dead. She wanted to end our family and it wouldn't matter if it happened after my birthday or not.

Tiptoeing downstairs, I took a long, loving gaze at the house. There was no denying that what I was about to do was dangerous. It was a very real possibility I would not, in fact, make it to my eighteenth birthday.

I saw George and Jackson standing on the stairs and offered them brave smiles. Ignoring the looks of hopelessness and sadness they wore, I turned towards the front door.

Hearing voices outside, I paused before opening it and peeked out the side window. There were eight or so reporters waiting with their cameras. A couple even held microphones. I moved before they could see me and hit my head gently against the wall in disbelief. This could not be happening.

I hastily snuck out the back. It bothered me, seeing them camped out on the lawn, hoping to catch a glimpse of the girl who may or may not be a witch. The press would believe anything if it sold more copies.

Jason and I were meeting Abby at her house to lay low all day. The last thing we wanted was to be out in public any more than we had to right now.

They were already there and ready to dig into a huge pancake breakfast Abby's mom had made. Jason came over and kissed me, an act I didn't think I'd ever get used to. He laid his forehead on mine for a minute or two before leading me over to the table.

Over breakfast, I told them about the reporters. Jason's reaction was the same it had been last night, to have his people issue a statement. Again I told him we should wait. We had more important things to worry about today.

Abby seemed to read my mind because she said, "I can't believe we're going to attempt to trap and cleanse a possessed person tonight who has a penchant for physical harm. Jason told me about what happened last night."

"It all comes down to tonight. We can't back down. I just hope we can lure her to the cemetery."

Jason took my hand and stared at me hard. "I really want you to think this through. We can get Marietta out of the house without any harm coming to you. I have some great lawyers who would love to throw a crazy woman out of a pre-Civil War mansion. I'm not comfortable with you putting yourself in danger."

"You have no idea how much that means to me. I have to deal with this now. If Marietta leaves, Catherine is just going to go with her, or worse, find another host close to me. We have to make her go away for good. Not only for my sake, but Marietta's too. Catherine's driving her insane. I can't watch it anymore."

"You wouldn't be you, Quinn, if you weren't thinking of someone else," Abby said. "Besides, you're right about getting rid of Catherine once and for all. Maybe if we put her to rest she can finally find some peace."

"And more importantly," Jason added, "you can get on with your life."

Despite his cool demeanor, I got the distinct impression he was having a difficult time forcing himself to be calm about the situation. After witnessing Catherine's power last night, he probably wasn't looking forward to going up against her.

It was Abby who also brought up the other obstacle in our way tonight.

"Are you absolutely sure we can trust Anna there, Quinn? I mean, I'm not cold-hearted. I understand why she wants to be there. But, to be honest, I still don't trust her."

"Especially after the article in the paper," Jason added.

"I think that was all Suzie. You guys are only watching out for me and I appreciate that. Anna sent me a text earlier wanting me to meet her at Baubles this afternoon so she can talk to me. I'll see what she has to say."

"I'm going with you." I started to shake my head but he continued, "Don't shake your head at me, either. It kills me that I haven't been able to really do anything. Yesterday I felt so helpless watching Catherine attack you and hearing your screams. I hated that feeling."

"You help me more than you can possibly be aware of. I have to do this with Anna alone. Plus there is the possibility it really is a trap and there will be mass amounts of reporters there. Stay here, please. It won't take long. If you're there, it will distract her."

He didn't look happy but he reluctantly agreed.

Abby left for a while to run some errands, leaving us alone on the couch. He drew me into an embrace and, in a matter of fact way, said, "You're scared."

"I'd be silly if I pretended I wasn't."

He shifted so he could look me in the eye. "Quinn, I've never met anyone like you before. Being with you has been one of the best times of my life."

Here was the goodbye I'd been dreading. There were only a couple days of post-production left on his movie and then he'd be out of here. Even if something bad happened to me, whatever this was between Jason and I would be over. I wanted to make this easier on him.

"Jason, don't," I started. "I know what you're going to say and you're right. It's been great but, one way or another, this is going to end. We'd be smart to say our goodbyes now. It was a summer fling and it was great."

He started laughing and it confused me. I didn't see anything funny about what I just said.

"Do you really think I was working up to a 'thanks it's been great but see ya' kind of speech?" I nodded uncertainly and he held my face in his hands. "Well, I'm not. I was going to tell you that I'm falling hard for you. When the movie is over I'm sticking around for a while to see where this thing with us goes before I head to Colorado to see my parents."

At first I wasn't quite sure of what he said. Slowly, as it sank in, I became speechless. Something I never dared to dream of was suddenly close enough to reach out and touch. All I wanted was a chance with him under normal circumstances. Here he was giving me that chance, and a whole lot more.

"W—what about your career?"

He flashed his dimples and shrugged. "It's not going anywhere. I can take some time off, help you get adjusted to life after Catherine."

"I haven't thought past my eighteenth birthday in weeks. It felt dangerous to dream about what comes afterwards. I could die tonight. You know that, right?"

"Yes, I do Quinn. I can't stop thinking about it. It's why I needed to tell you this now. You have so much to fight for. I would leave here with you today if you said the word and take you anywhere in the world you wanted to go. You'd be safe."

I started to speak but he continued, "But you won't do that. It's one of the things I admire about you. You'll do what's right for that crazy family of yours."

Hearing him say that, I knew I did love him. I think I'd loved him since the moment I saw him as the cocky actor with all the hidden layers. It only seemed to grow as I saw more and more of who he truly was.

So, why was admitting I felt the same way a more terrifying thought than the one of facing Catherine head on? I took a deep breath and let some of my emotions out. "I've got very strong feelings for you, too. You snuck in no matter how hard I tried to keep you out. I can't wait for this to be over and it's not hanging over our heads all the time."

We didn't really do much the rest of the day. We didn't have to meet Travis until nightfall so Jason and Abby did their best to keep me distracted. Still, it felt like a weight had lifted off my shoulders. Jason's declaration of love armed me for the battle I was walking into.

As I left to meet Anna, I only hoped it would be enough.

Chapter Thirty-Seven

After the article in the paper, I was reluctant to meet Anna but I wanted to ask if she had any idea how Suzie knew about me and Jason. In light of everything else going on, I realized it wasn't that important, but my curiosity was winning over. I thought we'd been so careful.

When I arrived at Baubles, she was already there surrounded by the remnants of ruined dresses. Even now, knowing it was Catherine, I got an uneasy feeling in the pit of my stomach. The amount of energy and hate put into doing this, well, it wasn't something I wanted to think about today of all days.

"Suzie is still absolutely convinced you did this." She looked up at me with a sad look on her face. "She and I are close in so many ways but lately I don't like who she's becoming."

I was unsure of what to say to her. For years, I'd witnessed the tight bond between them and never imagined anything getting in the way of that, especially me. I wanted to tell her it might only be a phase and not to give up on her sister, but I started to explain, she cut me off.

"I didn't have anything to do with the article, Quinn. I swear to you. Suzie didn't even tell me. I read it in the paper and it made me sick. I can't believe she did it. It was mean and uncalled for." She crossed her arms over her chest and asked, "So, is it true? About you and Jason Preston?"

She appeared genuine so I stepped closer to her and fingered a ripped swath of shiny fabric. Confiding in Abby had always been so easy. It was hard to get used to talking to someone else. I wanted to trust Anna.

"It is." I watched her eyes grow big. "I didn't want to care for him at first. He was arrogant and stubborn, but he wore me down. There's been a lot on my mind recently so I'm taking it one day at a time."

Telling her I loved him would be too much. I couldn't even tell him right now.

"Wow," Anna gushed. "You're so lucky. He's gorgeous. I met him once, just walking down the street. He was really nice and polite but I rambled on for, like, ever. I promise if we stay friends after this, I'll try not to drool."

"I want for us to be friends, Anna, but I'm afraid to give you too much. The last thing I want is for you to tell Suzie and have her running off to the reporters again. Plus, it's not as easy as I hoped it would be forgetting what you both put me through the last few years. In my heart, I've forgiven you. My mind warns me to still be careful."

"I completely understand. I don't blame you. We were pretty awful to you for so long. I hope one day soon we can get past it. I want to. We're not kids anymore."

Something came over me. I felt myself moving forward and giving her a tentative hug. Anna hesitated for a second before returning the gesture. It might be the first step towards a real friendship. I wasn't sure if I'd ever trust her a hundred percent, but at least we were headed in that direction.

I drew back and surveyed the room. "What's going to happen to all this stuff? The pageant is in a week, right?"

"Yeah, in eight days. I told Suzie I wasn't going to do it, that I never really wanted to in the first place. I've done pageants since I was five. I'm so over it. She, of course, threw a fit. She likes being in charge, being the alpha female. You know what I mean?" Anna shrugged. "She'll have to do it without me this time, if she can salvage anything."

It was impressive to see the changes in Anna over the last few weeks.

"Should we walk about tonight?" I asked her. I sensed we were both avoiding it.

She nodded reluctantly.

"Travis wants to keep you and Jason out of the way to make sure you're safe. I'm the only one who will be in harm's way. Travis said he might have to use you to give your mama a little jolt. I'll let him explain that later. It's going to be scary, Anna, but I promise Travis and Jason will do their best to keep you safe. You have to listen to them."

"Jason is going to be there?"

"Anna, you're going to have to concentrate on what is going on, not on Jason. He'll be there because he won't let me do it on my own. I think he's a lot more scared than he's letting on. He wanted me to run away."

"You're not the running away type. If you were, my sister and I would have run you off a long time ago. Even Mom was so mean to you, but I don't know how much of it can be blamed on this Catherine lady. And I promise I'll be all business tonight."

I checked the time on my cell phone.

"Alright, we should head back to Abby's and get Jason. Then we can head down to Colonial Park."

Anna followed me out and we walked in silence, each lost in our own thoughts.

I was more afraid because now I had so much to lose. Not only did I have a great guy who'd professed his love to me, I had taken the first steps towards gaining a sister.

Things were more complicated than ever.

Chapter Thirty-Eight

As darkness came, the living and non-living shadows woke to claim the streets and squares of the city. At night, Savannah looked much more populated than during the day. The cooler temperatures brought everyone out of their homes and hotel rooms to enjoy the fresh air, unless the heat still lingered stubbornly, as it did tonight.

The humidity clung to everything as the sun sank in the sky and there wasn't anyone milling around the cemetery as usual. I assumed Jason must have pulled a few more strings.

We met Travis at the entrance to Colonial Park. He carried a large backpack and a flashlight in his hand. His look was all business as he studied us. I introduced him to Anna, who'd been very quiet since leaving Abby's house.

"Are you guys ready? Are you sure you want to do this?" We all nodded. "Okay, just remember what I told you. All I need is to have her subdued. Hold her down, and then I can do the rest."

"Hold her down?" Anna squeaked.

Travis fixed his ice blue eyes on her. "I don't mean 'pin her down to the ground'. We only need to make sure she doesn't run away because if she leaves, Catherine leaves with her."

This seemed to satisfy Anna and she went back to glancing nervously at her surroundings.

Then he turned his stare to me and said, "Are you ready to make the call?" I nodded. "Good. Do whatever you can to stir her up enough so she'll come straight here."

I took a deep breath before making the call to Marietta. But instead of talking to her when she answered, I addressed Catherine and hoped it would work.

166

"Hello Catherine, its Quinn."

The long pause on the other end led me to believe I had gambled right.

"Quinn," she drew out my name in her dark, creepy drawl. "And to what do I owe the pleasure of your call?"

Here it goes.

"I know what you want and what you have planned for me. I'm willing to fight for what is mine; my house, my freedom, my life."

Her laugh sent chills shuddering through me. "Poor foolish Quinn, what makes you think you have the right to challenge me? I'm sure you remember how powerful I've grown."

"I'm well aware of your powers." I forced my voice to sound flippant, like I didn't care. "Why don't you come and meet me so we can finish this once and for all? I'm giving you the chance to make good on your threats."

"Have I given you reason to doubt me?" She sounded amused. I wasn't getting the reaction I'd hoped. "Why should I come to you?"

"I don't doubt you at all. I just want this to be over and I'm sure you do, too. Think about it Catherine, it will be you and me. You won't have your mother or Jackson swooping in to save me from you. As long as you come after me in that house, you won't win."

I waited through the silence, hoping I'd be able to lure her out of the house. I had felt her desire to have me dead and I was gambling everything on that.

"I promise you, I will finish you. I never got my happy ending and neither will you."

"Whatever, come to Colonial Park Cemetery. I'll be waiting at your grave. Unless you're too comfortable hiding behind such a weak woman."

"You'll regret that," she said with a growl.

I ended the call and dropped the phone. It was a miracle I'd been able to hold on to it that long. My hands were shaking badly and I had no control over them at all. Jason came over and put his hand in mine. Slowly, they stilled and I could breathe again.

"She's coming?" Travis asked.

All I could do was nod my head.

Chapter Thirty-Nine

I stood alone in the cemetery waiting for Catherine to arrive. Everyone else hid out of sight behind a row of tall tombstones. My palms were sweaty and my chest tightened as if it were in a vise.

It was too late to back out now. She was coming. One way or another, this was going to be over. Sure, I feared for my life but I'd almost become accustomed to it. What worried me was the lives of the others. I'd never forgive myself if anything happened to them.

Walking in a tight, nervous circle, I made note of the spirits and entities around me. On a rare whim, I opened my mind to them. I let them in, drawing in their desperation and their need. It temporarily distracted me and their emotions chased away my own.

I heard a footstep behind me, then another. It was Marietta. I knew it before I turned. Her face was blank, telling me that Catherine had full control. All I could do now was hope Anna stayed put.

Marietta stopped a few feet away from me but Catherine's shadow advanced closer.

"Well, well, look who has decided to show some courage. I'm almost impressed." The voice echoed through the clearing on its own. "Who would have thought? This won't end the way you hope, Quinn."

"I'm not hoping for anything. I just want some answers and for this to finally be over. I'm sick of constantly looking over my shoulder, waiting for you." It surprised me how strong my voice sounded considering I was trembling on the inside.

She seemed to consider this. "I think I can allow you a few questions before I end this."

That, I had not expected. As I thought about it, the darkness grew thicker and the air chilled. It was a hot, humid August night. It should have been stifling but goosebumps started appearing on my arms.

"Is Marietta okay?" Not the first question I thought would pop in my head.

I watched as slowly, Marietta came to and took note of her surroundings. Confusion flooded her face but it changed to fear as she realized where she was. Then she noticed me.

"Quinn?" she sobbed out. "How did I get here? What is going on?"

Not caring about how close Catherine was, I walked up to Marietta and grabbed her ice cold hands. "Are you okay?"

She was frightened half to death, her eyes darting frantically. Anna popped into my line of vision and my heart sank. Jason and Travis wrestled her back into place with one of their hands over her mouth.

Please stay quiet, I prayed.

"I-I don't know what's been going on." At last her eyes came to rest on mine. "I didn't mean to hurt you, Quinn. I saw what was happening but I couldn't do anything about it. When I told your daddy I would take care of you, I meant it. I didn't mean to do this to you."

Her words made me tear up. I hated crying at a moment when I needed to be my strongest. The desperation in her voice broke my heart

"I know it wasn't you doing those things."

"I've missed so much. I feel like I've been walking in a fog for months. I'm not even sure what day it is."

"Marietta, listen to me. I need to ask you something." Her crazed eyes landed on me again and I asked in a soothing voice. "What did you promise her? Why did you let her do this to you?"

Frantically, she shook her head in quick motions. "She said she would help me become a more important member of society, that she knew how badly I wanted it. I was distraught after your father died and didn't want to be a single mother to three teenage girls. Two were bad enough. She said she'd make sure you were out of the picture. I never thought she meant for you to die. I swear I didn't."

She became hysterical and tried to get away from me. I desperately wanted to help her but Catherine interfered. Before I could even blink an eye, the vacant stare came back and Marietta was gone. Her body sagged in my arms.

"Just let her be!"

Laughter came from every direction. "I'm getting bored. Ask your questions so we can be done with this."

I tried to collect myself. Seeing Marietta in that state scared me to death. I couldn't move or speak. Breathing became more difficult. Wanting everything to over, I brought out a question I hoped would agitate her.

"How does it feel to know you're no better than William Jennings?"

That ticked her off royally.

Catherine came at me with more force and more ferocity than she ever had before. She would have knocked me off my feet but my body was already so tense, I only wobbled. The overpowering oppression deepened and soon numbness crept over me until every muscle became paralyzed.

Then, the pain came.

Acute and everywhere, it flashed through me so fast I lost all rational thought. I let out a raw, primal scream. I was aware that Travis held Jason back while Abby and Anna clung to each other as they watched in horror.

I was frozen in place, but I tried to keep an eye on what was going on around me. Catherine had not lessened her hold on me, which meant she must not be aware of Jason or Travis and what we were attempting.

But the minute they made a move on Marietta, that changed. Though I still could not move, the pain dulled. I heard Catherine roar in anger as she realized someone was holding Marietta's body in place.

"You are fools if you think this is going to work on me."

She kept her shadow between me and them. Jason ran forward, but immediately he was thrown back into a tombstone. The tombstone shattered and Abby raced over to his side.

"Catherine Roberts!" Travis yelled. "You do not belong in this place. Go and find your peace. Leave this woman alone."

Catherine laughed coldly in response. "Your parlor tricks are no use here."

To emphasize her point, the pain intensified to an almost unbearable level. I struggled as hard as I could to hold on, to find some way to fight her but I was losing the battle.

Somewhere, in the agonized jumble of thoughts, one slipped through.

I won't let you do this.

Oh, Quinn, you're such a sad, pathetic girl. Think of all you have to lose.

A vision of kissing Jason at the ball burned bright in front of my eyes. For a brief second, I forgot the pain and the paralysis gripping me. All I saw was the affection in Jason's eyes and felt my love for him burst out and try to fight Catherine back. Unfortunately, my energy was draining fast and holding onto the image was impossible.

It was gone as quick as it came.

Yes, he is delicious. I can see why you would think he's worth sticking around for. In fact, I don't really want to kill you anymore.

Fear's cold hand closed on my heart.

What do you mean? I asked.

The pain flared inside me and she refused to release me. I heard Travis ordering her to let go of her earthly bonds. Off to the side, Jason pulled himself

170

to his feet and grimaced in pain. He begged Catherine to let me go. I wasn't sure where Abby or Anna went but I knew they were close because I heard Anna pleading with Marietta. Wind buffeted the entire area like we were stuck in the middle of a hurricane.

Still, I waited and nothing changed.

Right when I thought it couldn't get any worse, it intensified even more. Like once before, the cold oily substance making up her shadow forced its way down my throat. It seeped into every inch of my body. Then, it had a hold of me and withdrew. Only when it withdrew, it pulled my insides along with it.

If I hadn't been in so much pain, I would've been able to make more sense of the sucking sensation. She was taking the life right out of me.

Jason must have noticed the change in what she was doing because he tried once again to get to me. "Quinn, don't you dare give up. Fight!"

I watched as his body lifted off the ground and held, suspended in the air. He struggled but was as trapped as me.

Don't, I managed to get one word across. His words gave me hope and I fought back against the darkness invading me. I pictured his feelings for me as a light I carried within me and imagined it replacing all the darkness penetrating me. To that, I added the love and the bright memories from my childhood.

For a while, it worked. I was able to move my mouth and scream out one word. "Jason!"

Catherine's laugh echoed in my head and steeled my determination, but she fought harder and this time it was worse. The sucking and the ripping didn't stop and I sensed Catherine's power growing even more. Her shadow swelled and overwhelmed me. Love and happiness were my only weapons and I battered against her, pushing against whatever was trying to shatter my soul. I wasn't going to let her take everything from me. Even though I was running out of options and losing consciousness, I ignored the temptation of letting go. Letting go meant failing my mama, even my daddy, along with all our ancestors. It had to end here, now.

I'll never let you win.

Those were the last words I managed as the blackness took me, once and for all.

Epilogue

I woke up in the attic, disorientated and alone.

The last thing I remembered was Catherine rushing at me and the sickening sensation of being ripped apart. I heard Jason scream my name. And then everything went black.

Cautiously, I sat up and peered around. Something was different.

There were piles of junk everywhere but my stuff was missing. It felt emptier, like no one had stepped foot up here for weeks.

I sniffed.

It even smelled musty and locked up.

I stood up from the bed and instantly felt light-headed. I had to reach out to steady myself on the desk. Something was wrong.

Even walking to the door was a challenge. I must have been out longer than I thought because I had a hard time putting one foot in front of the other.

The attic door was open and I took my time going down the stairs. When my foot touched the landing the air felt cleaner, fresher. This part of the house felt lived in and I vaguely wondered if Marietta and the twins were home.

Maybe what we attempted to do in the park didn't work. The second I thought that, my palms grew wet and my stomach plunged.

No, I couldn't consider that. It had to have worked.

As I walked past the twins rooms, I saw they were empty. Marietta's room wasn't, but it was filled with furniture and things I didn't recognize.

A cold knot formed in my stomach.

What was going on?

On the first floor, the rooms were different as well. The living room furniture was new, so was the large plasma TV. If I didn't know better, I would have thought I was in someone else's home.

I heard movement behind me. Half expecting to see a random stranger, I was surprised to see George. Not because it was George, but because I could *see* him.

No longer was he just a faint image from the corner of my vision or an almost transparent figure. Standing before me was a real live War era slave boy. I knew that if I reached out and touched him, I would feel him.

"George, what's happened?"

He was about to cry. In a sad, desperate whisper he said my name, "Quinn."

What made it so unbelievable was I heard him with my ears, not just in my head.

I was about to ask him more when the front door opened and Jason walked in laughing. Before I could run up to him and throw my arms around him, I saw who he was laughing with.

It was me.

Only it wasn't.

The girl with Jason looked like me, but had such a look of happiness and love I felt envious of her. Her hair was a little shorter than mine and layered. She even wore makeup.

I watched, unable to move a muscle as Jason bent down and kissed her passionately. It stole my breath away. Not because I knew what his kisses felt like. It stole my breath away because somehow I knew it went horribly wrong in the cemetery that night.

"Jason," I squeaked.

He didn't answer or even turn in my direction so I tried again louder.

"Jason!"

Still *nothing*.

I walked over and laid my hand on his arm but it didn't touch him. It passed through him as if he wasn't even there.

I didn't have a chance to gather my frayed thoughts. The girl who was not me turned around and lifted her lip in a sneer. Then, she winked at me and laid a newspaper on the table in the foyer.

On the front page was a picture of Jason and me, smiling for the cameras in front of a restaurant. The headline read, "Jason Preston falls for local girl." My head pounded from trying to catch up with what was going on until I saw the date.

If I was looking at today's paper, it had been sixteen days since my eighteenth birthday.

Finally, my thoughts caught up and the horrible truth slammed into me.

It hadn't worked and, to make matters worse, Catherine had taken over my body. I went to chase after them as they walked holding hands into the kitchen.

George came up beside me and I *felt* his hand on my arm holding me back as real and solid as a living person.

"Let me go. I have to warn him."

George shook his head with a sad smile. "You can't. You're one of us now."

Then, the sick realization of what happened settled over me, oily and dirty. I was a ghost, a thin wisp of who I used to be. Catherine had found a way to inhabit my body, which meant it *was* possible. As quickly as that thought struck home, however, stubborn determination replaced it. She'd stolen my body, my home and most of all, the man I loved. I couldn't stand the thought of losing Jason so soon after I'd found him. I had to find a way to get him back, to get it *all* back. Catherine unjustly held it for now, but not forever. I was *not* going to let her win. Someday, somehow, I would find a way to get my life back, and when I did, Catherine would be history.

Literally.

About the Author

Missy Fleming lives in beautiful Bozeman, Montana where her love of being outdoors often conflicts with her love of writing. Luckily, winter makes it a little easier. Missy contributes to multiple writing sites and Happily Never After is her first published novel in the United States. She is blessedly single, dedicating her affections to travel, writing, reading, family and her six year old Bichon Frise, Jack.

Coming soon!
A Strange There After
Book 2 of the Savannah Shadows Series